STRANGE
BUSINESS

STRANGE
BUSINESS
Rilla Askew

VIKING

VIKING
Published by the Penguin Group
Viking Penguin, a division of Penguin Books USA Inc.,
375 Hudson Street, New York, New York 10014, U.S.A.
Penguin Books Ltd, 27 Wrights Lane, London W8 5TZ, England
Penguin Books Australia Ltd, Ringwood, Victoria, Australia
Penguin Books Canada Ltd, 10 Alcorn Avenue, Suite 300,
Toronto, Ontario, Canada M4V 3B2
Penguin Books (N.Z.) Ltd, 182–190 Wairau Road,
Auckland 10, New Zealand

Penguin Books Ltd, Registered Offices:
Harmondsworth, Middlesex, England

First published in 1992 by Viking Penguin,
a division of Penguin Books USA Inc.

1 3 5 7 9 10 8 6 4 2

Publisher's Note
This is a work of fiction. Names, characters, places, and incidents either
are the product of the author's imagination or are used fictitiously, and
any resemblance to actual persons, living or dead, events, or locales is
entirely coincidental.

Portions of this novel first appeared as short stories in *Carolina Quarterly, Cottonwood Magazine, Iris, North Dakota Quarterly,* and *Sonora
Review.*

LIBRARY OF CONGRESS CATALOGING IN PUBLICATION DATA
Askew, Rilla.
Strange business / Rilla Askew.
p. cm.
ISBN 0–670–84259–1
I. Title.
PS3551.S545S7 1992   91–40955
813'.54—dc20

Printed in the United States of America
Set in Primer

For Jody Read, who helped me
once, long ago, to finish,
and for Paul, who helped me
begin

Contents

STRANGE
BUSINESS

the night, never let out a sound. They all thought Holbird was dead, but he was just stunned and come to afterwhile and they rode on west again.

But they all knew that to be a bad sign. No panther jumps on a man riding with eight other men and horses.

When they got to Joe Hokolutubbee's they found him sleeping on the porch. Silan Lewis went in first. He went in close enough to see the outline of Joe's body on a bed there in the corner. Joe must've heard him. Who is it? he called out in the dark. Joe sat up, said it again. Who is it? Who's there? Silan Lewis never answered. He fired one shot. That signaled the others and everybody went in firing. They shot Joseph Hokolutubbee all to pieces there on the dark porch. He never even got up from the bed.

Then they rode on again.

Rode fast.

Rode west towards McAlester.

They were set to kill three or four others. They believed that all over the Three Districts other Choctaws were carrying out their executions in the night, same way they'd all made it up together. But it didn't happen like that.

Somebody must've told. Time they got to McAlester, the men they were set to execute were all hiding out. They couldn't find nobody to kill. A fella rode in from Tuskahoma and told how all over the Nation the Progressives were either lined up to fight or else hiding out like rabbits. So they knew there was some serious trouble.

They had a standoff there at McAlester for a time. Both sides come together and faced off at McAlester, men from both parties camped out west of town. They sat looking at each other, hundreds of armed Choctaws ready to fight and kill one another. They sat that way for four days.

They never did fight. That's one part of this story.

They started in talking. Afterwhile they finally settled that they'd break up and go home to their families, and Silan Lewis and his bunch would go to trial for the death of Deputy Sheriff Joseph Hokolutubbee.

So the men who rode with Silan Lewis surrendered.

Silan himself was getting his horse shod one cold morning in South McAlester, and Tecumseh Moore come along and nodded his head at him. Silan paid off the blacksmith and saddled up his red mare, mounted her, followed Moore back to Hartshorne, where the other riders were under guard. The two were quiet on the way from McAlester to Hartshorne. They neither one said a word. Tecumseh Moore kept his back to Silan Lewis, walked his horse slow in the dirt of the road.

So it come about there was a trial. A lot of talk, a lot of words in the newspapers. The United States government come in on it. The papers took sides and stirred up the people. Each side called the other Buzzards and Skunks.

Choctaw court said the men who killed Joe Hokolutubbee had to be shot. Some of the people said that was right. Others said no, they ought to only receive one hundred lashes. But the court said they had to be shot.

The United States government come in on it again.

There was more trials and papers and lawyering.

Come down to only Silan Lewis and one other was set to be executed.

Come down to it finally, Silan Lewis was the only one they said had to be shot.

So Silan Lewis went back home to wait for the day of his execution. He stayed home for one season and a little more, and then after harvest and just before winter and more than two years after the death of Joe Hokolutubbee, Silan Lewis hitched up his team and set out from the house with his wife sitting silent and staring in the wagon beside him.

There were some in the Nation had already forgot the old ways.

They tried to talk Silan Lewis into running. Said he ought to keep going in that wagon and head on down into Texas. Said it was no sense anymore in a man traveling headlong to his own death. But Silan Lewis kept to the old ways. The shame was going to kill him if he went down to Texas, so there he'd be dead anyhow but with shame and not honor. It wasn't any kind of choice for a man. Him and his wife drove twenty miles in one day and set up camp near the courthouse alongside the creek.

Now, Tecumseh Moore let it be known about that if anybody wanted to rescue Silan Lewis, why, him and his men would give him up without a fight. That would happen sometimes back in those days, a man who was set to get executed might get took off on horseback by his friends just before he got shot. Most of the people thought that would happen with Silan Lewis. Choctaw government thought it would happen and that's how come them to send in the lighthorsemen. They were swarming around all over the place. Tecumseh Moore thought it would happen. He believed it would happen. He didn't want to shoot his old friend.

He waited past the time when the sun reached its high point. That was the time set for the execution. The day was a color like the breast of a mourning dove, grayish-like brown shaded nearly to pink. Tecumseh Moore acted like he couldn't see when the sun reached its high point, but the sun was one light spot trying to burn through the skymist and anybody could see it. He had them read the death sentence two or three times. The lighthorsemen pranced their horses in and out amongst the people. The people talked in low voices, and then their voices started rising like the slow rise of wind.

Tecumseh Moore could see there wasn't any help for it. He said, I'm not going to shoot this man, we've been friends all my life. He appointed Deputy Sheriff Lyman Pusley to do the shooting, and sent for the blanket.

They spread the blanket according to law on the ground at the side of the courthouse. The people gathered in a great circle all around. Silan Lewis took off his jacket and sat on the blanket. He didn't look at his wife. Didn't look at anybody, just stared between the legs of the people at the courthouse wall straight ahead. His wife stood inside the circle of people. She didn't act like anything but looked across to the other side of the circle with eyes like a blind woman. Eli Holbird took Silan's boots off him. He was the only one of the eight men who helped him kill Joe Hokolutubbee to show up for his execution. Least he was the only one anybody saw. Holbird held Silan's boots and went over and stood in the circle next to Silan's wife.

One Choctaw man stretched Silan Lewis's legs out in front of him on the blanket. Silan sat up straight. Two others held Silan's arms stretched out on either side of him. Another man walked up behind him and bent over his shoulder and opened his shirt. The shirt was white. This man dipped his fingers in a tin of white powder and put his fingers on Silan Lewis's chest and drew a white circle over the place he figured Silan's heart to be. Silan kept his eyes open and steady on the wall of the courthouse. He sat stiff, his shirt and the powdered circle glaring white, answering each other against the brown of his skin.

Tecumseh Moore looked up the road and down the road. His eyes searched the hills cradling the courthouse on all sides. The people were silent like wind that drops and goes still in the last minute before a twister. There was no sound of horses running. No movement on the road or among the oaks and cedars on the hills. Sheriff Moore waited for some sign of rescue. The pale disk of sun slid long past the high point, and there was no sound. Lyman Pusley held his Winchester ready. Sheriff Moore raised his arm finally, and still there was no movement.

Then a high keening cry came, first light and faraway-sounding so that the sheriff didn't know where it came from, and then close by, high-pitched, tortured, with no stops for breath in between. It came from the closed lips and dead eyes of Silan Lewis's white wife.

Tecumseh Moore swooped his arm down.

Lyman Pusley fired his rifle.

Smoke puffed from the mouth of the rifle, and the white circle on Silan Lewis's chest exploded into red. He jerked back and sprawled face up, arms open, on the blanket. Those two Choctaws still had hold of his hands.

But Silan Lewis wasn't dead yet.

His wife's high cry dropped low and snarling in her belly like the growl of a hurt dog. Silan Lewis jerked and twitched on the blanket, and the two men held him down by the arms. The people watched, silent, and one or two of them walked away.

Still Silan Lewis wouldn't die.

Tecumseh Moore looked at him twitching on the blanket, not living and not dying. Silan Lewis made no sound.

After too much time passed, Sheriff Moore knew again that there wasn't any help for it. He went over and knelt on the blanket. He put the palm of his left hand over the mouth of his friend, and felt the warm breath pushing against it. Silan's eyes were glazed over, but he turned them from the sky to look up at Tecumseh Moore's eyes.

Sheriff Tecumseh Moore saw it then.

He saw it like a memory he'd nearly forgotten.

How there was no reason for the people to be all turned against themselves and killing each other. How Silan Lewis had no call to shoot Joe Hokolutubbee in his bed on his dark porch. How Lyman Pusley had no call to shoot Silan Lewis. How in the old time in the old Nation, in the homeland where the bones of the ancestors were buried, in *okla falaya* by the Tombigbee waters, in the long-ago time the Choctaw knew how to fight and kill enemies. How enemies were always, in the old time, only others and not the Choctaw people themselves.

And how it was when the white man wanted the land of the old Nation that the people first came to be divided. How the white man said to some of them, here, you give us this land and we'll give you this other, and it will belong to the Choctaw as long as the waters run. How the white man had a good trick then to give whiskey to some and money to others, how he'd name some of them chiefs who had no right or honor to be named so, for the one purpose of getting those Choctaws to sign papers of lies giving away the people's land. How it was the people divided that was the first sign of the loss of the old Nation, before so many died on the long trail of tears when the people left the bones of the old ones and came up the great river, removed by the white soldiers to the new land.

Tecumseh Moore felt the warm living breath of Silan Lewis, felt him jerking and shaking.

He closed the fingers of his right hand over the nose of Silan Lewis and squeezed shut the air holes and twisted his palm into Silan Lewis's mouth. Silan's eyes stayed open, looking up at the eyes of my grandfather, and his twitches and spasms grew slower and softer. My grandfather knew then that he knelt on the death blanket with his killing hand on his friend's mouth because the Choctaw had not known how to turn back that good trick of the white man. They hadn't known how to keep him from turning the people against themselves.

So not long after the death of Silan Lewis the United States government passed the law allowing allotments and carved up the Nation. Not too long after that the land was all gone out of the people's hands. Like some of 'em said, it wasn't any choice anyhow.

Well, this story's an old one.

It happened a long time ago.

Back when our words *okla humma* that called us the red people had not yet turned over to mean white man's land.

Hamp Humphrey's small white frame house sat just back from the footpath that led into town. In summer we traipsed up and down that footpath a dozen times a day on milk-and-bread errands for our mothers or penny-nail errands for our fathers or the more important business of trudging up to Sanger's gas station on the highway for candy bars and pop. Always on our back-and-forth journeys we'd find Hamp Humphrey sitting in his great iron lawn chair under the elm tree in his front yard. It never mattered about the weather: on the haziest, hottest dog day in August old Hamp would still be there, fanning himself feebly with a cardboard church fan on a stick. The rasping voices of locusts in his elm tree would make the air seem to weigh more, and Hamp would slur out a greeting to us as we passed. Most of us would stop and shake hands, not only for the good reason that we'd been taught that way but also because our small fists would come away from the encounter clutching shiny nickels and dimes, placed there by the great palsied red slabs of Hamp Humphrey's hands.

Some of the younger children were afraid of Hamp and would cross over to the far side of the road and walk in the drainage ditch rather than pass his house alone, but most of us understood him to be harmless, just a large uncomfortable man with quaking hands and a thick, slurring tongue. Some of us had heard through the whispers in our kitchens that he'd gotten that way from falling off a house when he was a boy. Some said, no it wasn't a house, it was a horse. Some said, oh yeah, you're full of baloney, I know from my daddy good and well it was a tractor; others said oil rig; still others swore he had been injured in the war. The only thing any of us understood for certain was that he'd been born normal and some unaccountable accident in life had turned him into the thing he'd become.

Hamp's body was soft and egg-shaped, his head a smooth oval crisscrossed with sparse yellow hairs. His face, in summer or winter, was a heavy, dull reddish color and his tongue lolled out thick and red between his lips when he spoke. We could not make anything of his words—just long, drawn-out moaned words made of nothing but vowels—but we knew from experience to nod and say, yes sir, Mr. Hamp sir, it surely is warm today, when we stood in front of his chair waiting to shake his hand. He held his head cocked always a little to the side and folded down on his chest, and when we agreed with him about the weather he would smile and wag it sadly from side to side.

Hamp's hands were the same dull red color as his face and they, like everything else about him, were mushy and soft-looking, rounded in all the places where our fathers had calluses and knuckles and knots. They quavered and quaked when he held them at rest, and when he moved one of them to reach for our small palms, it danced a slow tortuous rhythm toward us and then stood in the air, weaving delicately back and forth, until our hands caught up to it. Few of us had ever seen Hamp Humphrey walk—he seemed always to just be there, morning or evening, out front in his big iron lawn chair, fanning himself with his worn-out church fan—but those of us who had happened by at the telling moment spoke in awed whispers of how he dragged one whole leg behind him and had to pull himself up onto the porch with his wavering hands. We speculated often about how he got on alone in his house and went to the bathroom and ate dinner and all. Our dependence on our own mothers made Hamp's independence more awesome and strange.

But all of us accepted Hamp Humphrey, as we accepted Mrs. Rainer's weak-witted daughter who sat on a milk crate on the Rainers' front porch rocking back and forth all night and all day, as we accepted Pete Ketchworth's drunkenness and Stump Wil-

son's missing arm and the five-legged calf that got born on the
Duvall place one spring. Such aberrations could not be aberrations in a town so small as ours, where our parents knew all the
secret histories and so understood which sorrows were a case of
the sins of the fathers being visited upon the sons and which a
case of direct divine retribution and which merely a result of the
mysterious ways of the Lord. We were children and had been
trained up strictly in the way we should go, so that we did not
think to question any earthly thing it was in the will of our parents
to accept.

The journey past Hamp Humphrey's house was part of growing
up in Cedar. His life was the mystery of our childhood, secret
and wonderful and strange, but going past his house marked
things out for us in ways without words so that we knew always
where we stood. We did not speak about it, never said the words
openly, but it was known that when you were old enough and
unafraid enough to walk directly up to his lawn chair and shake
hands with him like a grownup and take your nickel away with
you to spend on a candy bar at Sanger's, you were old enough
to be accepted on your own terms and not just as so-and-so's
little brother or sister. Likewise, there was a point when you were
too old to stop by Hamp Humphrey's. Anyone who continued to
go by there after all the rest of us knew the time had passed (and
no one knew how we knew and it was another thing we never
spoke about) would be subject to bad persecutions because that
was almost as disgraceful as going trick-or-treating after you'd
gotten too big.

The whispers began, as most whispers began, in somebody's
kitchen. We children could not find out the details of the story,
only that it had to do with something Gladys Holloway said.
Gladys Holloway was not one of us children but an older girl, not
quite yet a woman, who did not go to school but cleaned people's
houses instead. The Holloways were not really one of the bad

families and not quite one of the good families—they traversed some kind of shifting no man's land in between. But people felt sorry for Gladys because her mother had died when she was little and none of the rest of the Holloways would take her. She'd been raised all alone by her daddy and had become shy and sullen and some folks said sneaky from so many beatings and so much time spent alone. Our parents made certain to hire her if they needed someone to houseclean and paid her fair wages because that was the kind of charity our parents did—but they also made certain to be home when she came to clean and watched to make sure her sweater was no more bulky when she walked out the door than when she walked in.

But Gladys Holloway said something to somebody. Some of our mothers said, oh fiddlesticks, I don't believe a word of it, it's downright impossible, anybody could see that. (These were words our mothers would let us hear in their kitchens, though the words that Gladys Holloway had said were sealed behind thin, pressed-tight lips whenever we came in.) But others shook their heads and said, I don't know, I don't know. Our fathers stayed out of it at first and only cautioned their own womenfolk to not let the word of a Holloway be taken as gospel. But the whispers kept on, and Gladys Holloway never went to Hamp Humphrey's house to clean anymore.

We cared as little as our fathers for the whispers at first. They had no more to do with our lives than the rustles and murmurs and low breathy sighs we'd heard when Sissy Wilson went away very fat in the belly and came back skin and bones and crying all the time. The faint susurrous sounds belonged to the walls of our mothers' kitchens in the same way that the tree frogs outside our windows belonged to the night. Our lives went on in their small important ways and it wasn't until our mothers began taking us aside, one by one, to caution us about going by Hamp Humphrey's that we picked up our heads and paid attention to the whispers and began to try to find out what they were all about.

We gathered in the schoolyard or down by the creek to tell each other our mothers' words and brag about the whispers we'd overheard and question and wonder at just what the words meant. We pretended to each other to know a great deal. The youngest ones became terrified of Hamp Humphrey and cried often and would not walk by there, even on the far side of the road. But the rest of us were not so much afraid as contemptuous. Hadn't he always been a soft, mushy man? Hadn't he always seemed to us like a great soft-boiled egg or something squishy and useless and red? We went by Hamp Humphrey's yard, never along the path but out in the middle of the road, and stared at him and wondered at how he could have done such a thing (and somebody said their mother had said he had Thrown Her Down, Actually Thrown Her Down, such a terrible, impossible thing, and our small bodies quaked in the night when we were alone and not so brave to think of being Thrown Down by those quavering hands). Some of the older ones catcalled at Hamp Humphrey and used words they'd heard from the walls of their kitchens or made up words of their own, but most of us just walked by and stared.

Hamp continued on in his lawn chair, every morning, every evening, and now when we came by he would lift his bobbing head from his chest and look at us, and when we paused in our journey to gaze at him he would lift one twitching arm and let it dance a spasmodic greeting in the air. We thought ourselves to be quite courageous, walking so near Hamp Humphrey's house, and it became a mark of great stature and bravery to step close to the path or Hamp's overgrown yard.

Still, he sat every day in his lawn chair, and our mothers began to click tongues over such a disgrace. Somebody should speak to him, they said to our fathers, someone was going to have to have a talk with him, that much was clear. Our fathers, who had ducked their heads and picked their teeth and spent more time at their work since the whispers began, started talking to each other. So long resistant to the power of the whispers, they now took them in their mouths and voiced them and changed them, and the words gained strength and anger as they spoke them out loud. *Somebody* was going to have to talk to him. They talked to each other over fence posts and in barnyards, at the gas station and feed store, in the yard of the church. They delegated authority, and then took it back again or the delegate shook it off. They discussed and discussed the Hamp Humphrey situation, and we children, playing nearby, listened to the words that they said.

And so it was that on the last morning in August, our last morning of freedom before school the next day, we gathered by unspoken agreement in the roadway in front of Hamp Humphrey's house. We said to each other, very grownup and disgusted, well, *somebody* is just going to have to speak to him, that's all there is to it, and we spat in the dust and shook our heads.

Hamp called to us from his lawn chair, and his words drooled out long and useless and slurring in the humid air. Somebody said, go see what he wants, and we pushed at each other and dug our toes in the roadbed, but finally, all together, as if by some signal, we crossed the roadway and waded through the weeds in his yard to stand bunched together at a safe distance in front of his chair. Hamp went on trying to talk to us, his great heavy head lifted off of his chest, his pale eyes watching us and his thick tongue pushing the words without form or consonants or reason out from his lips. We listened for a long time, and watched him. His face was darkened in the shade of the elm tree. His hands were trapped like two wayward things, locked together, between his knees. After a while his tongue went silent, and the rising falling rising song of the locusts wrapped all around us and weighed down the air. Hamp sat looking at us, his head bobbing wearily from the strain of keeping it lifted off his chest.

Somebody said, yes sir, Mr. Hamp, it's a hot day today sure enough, and for one flickering moment no time had passed and it was all as it had ever been. Hamp's lips pulled jerkily to one side in a smile, and he wagged his sorrowful agreement.

And then somebody laughed, and we all began laughing, and Hamp's hands flew loose from their captured place between his knees. He began digging in his loose pockets for money, and we all grew silent and watchful, and when he pulled a quaking hand filled with coins free from his pocket, we put our hands behind our backs and started walking backwards, backing away. Hamp called to us again and the words were like the lowing of a calf for its mother or the moan of a lost hound dog in the night. And so somebody laughed again, and we all joined in laughing, a nervous staccato peppering the air.

Hamp tried to stand up then, and we knew in an instant that he was coming for us, to reach out for us with those terrible hands and Throw Us Down. Some of the younger ones screamed, and we all started running, and when we had nearly reached town, our breaths bursting in our chests, we turned and looked back. We could see the enormous soft body of Hamp Humphrey lying in the weeds beside his chair, arms and legs waving, useless and senseless, like a turned-over insect on the ground.

The next morning Skeet Johnson came around to deliver Hamp's groceries and called and called through the latched screen door. He told us all how it happened, how he finally set the sacks down on the porch and went around back to check and found Hamp laying there face-up on the concrete slab of the storm cellar in the back yard. How Hamp's back was broken but he wasn't dead yet and how he just laid there and moaned and kept trying to move his pitiful arms. How Skeet had to put his fist through the screen of the back door to call the ambulance and how they liked to never got him up on the stretcher, he was the same as dead weight. How it was Skeet's own opinion that Hamp must have got up on the rooftop some way, there couldn't be no other explanation for it, not with a broken back and all, but how you could explain both doors being locked from the inside was a mystery to him that might not never be explained.

It took Hamp Humphrey six days to die. All the long while he was dying, our fathers gathered in the churchyard or the parking lot of the hospital and shook their heads, saying, it's strange-eyed to me, that's a fact, but looks to me like somebody should have gone over there and had a talk with the man. Our mothers whispered in their kitchens, don't tell me, I knew good and well it was possible, if he could get himself up on that rooftop, he was capable of anything, there's just no telling what all he might would have done.

We children just never looked at each other when they talked about Hamp Humphrey. Some of us said sometimes, see, I *told* you it was a fall off a house. And somebody said one time, don't you think he could have crawled around back there from where he was laying in the front yard? and the rest of us shouted, you're crazy! that don't give you a broken back! In our minds we saw him sitting on the edge of the rooftop, his quaking soft hands moving in the moonlight and his bobbling head nodding up and down. We knew he was too soft to smash like a brittle insect or the shell of an egg, and that's why he had to lay there all night, paralyzed and dying, but unable to die.

1964

C ephus Sumpter loved his cousin Harriman, and he loved Harriman's pet coon. In the afternoons when Granny Ryder lay down for her nap, Cephus would slip out the back door. He'd take off across the yard, dancing fast to keep out of the way of the chickens, and walk down the two-lane track to the cattleguard and stand there, staring across the road at his cousin Harriman's house. Cephus never crossed the cattleguard by himself. Harriman had told him there was boogers down there who'd eat him up in a minute if he accidentally let a foot slip through one of the cracks. Harriman knew more about boogers and banshees and ghosts than even Granny Ryder herself, so Cephus took him at his word and never tried crossing the guard on his own. He'd only just stand there, a safe distance back from the secret darkness between the slats, and watch.

After a while, sure enough, the yellow school bus would come over the hill and stop in the road and spit Harriman and the three Slakeman children out into the dust. Cephus would wait until the Slakemans had started up the hill to their house, and then he'd call across the road, "Ha-a-arriman. Ha-a-arriman."

Sometimes Harriman heard him and came over and lifted him up and carried him across the wooden slats. He'd set him down in the dirt then and take hold of his hand and walk him across the road to the cattleguard on the other side. He'd pick him up and carry him across that one and set him down again, and together they'd climb the hill to Harriman's house.

If Harriman's ma was in a good mood, she might phone across the road to Granny Ryder and ask could Cephus stay to supper. And sometimes Granny Ryder was in a good mood and said that would be all right. Then Harriman and Cephus would stay out on the back porch and play with Harriman's pet coon until Harriman's ma called them in to eat.

Harriman would take Cephus back across the road just before dark, and Cephus would wash up and go to bed happy.

Some days the school bus only spit out the Slakemans because Harriman stayed late after school to play ball. Some days it rained. Some days Harriman would act like he hadn't heard Cephus at all when he stood in his place by the cattleguard calling, "Ha-a-arriman. Ha-a-arriman." Harriman would just nod at the Slakemans and turn and go up the hill, no matter how loud Cephus called. He wouldn't look back. He'd just open the screen and go on in the house.

Those nights in particular Cephus cried in his bed and wished he was big enough for school or to play ball or to have a pet coon or to show Harriman something.

Harriman's coon was named Rowdy. Harriman's pa had shot Rowdy's ma on a coon hunt, and when she fell dead out of the tree, Rowdy had been clinging to her back. Harriman's pa called the dogs off and picked Rowdy up and put him in a canvas bag and brought him home for Harriman to raise. Harriman kept him in a rain barrel turned on its side. An old icebox grate stood in front of the mouth to keep Rowdy from getting out, and two concrete blocks stood in front of the grate. Rowdy was pretty strong for a coon and had ripped right through the chicken wire Harriman had put up in the first place. Harriman kept three flat metal pans outside the rain barrel: one to hold Rowdy's food, one to hold his drinking water, and a third one—also full of water— for Rowdy to wash his food in before he ate it.

Harriman said coons were the smartest animals in the wild because they knew they were supposed to wash their food before they ate it.

Harriman's ma said somebody might think they was smart and somebody might think they was clean but that was the stinkingest animal she'd ever laid eyes on and it didn't know how to do a thing in the world but make stinking messes.

Rowdy knew how to do one thing, a trick Harriman had taught him. Harriman would put peanuts or grapes or lettuce leaves in any one of his eight overalls pockets and sit down on the edge of the porch. Rowdy would crawl around picking at Harriman's pockets until he found the right one, then he'd dig in the pocket with his tiny black fingers and pull out the food. Cephus loved to watch Rowdy do that.

Sometimes Harriman would put a grape in Cephus's pocket and let Rowdy hunt there. Cephus stood very still when Rowdy hunted in his pockets, and it was like when Granny Ryder washed him up for Sunday School and slicked his hair and checked his ears and picked and pulled at his collar and buttons. It was like having somebody mess with him. As soon as Rowdy found something—no matter even if it was a peanut in a shell—he'd carry it over to one of the water pans and wash it. He didn't care that one pan was for drinking and the other for washing, he'd just go to whichever pan was closest and turn the particle of food over and over in the water with his two little hands.

Harriman said that proved how smart coons was because Rowdy was just a bitty baby when Harriman got him, and Harriman never taught him how to do that. He taught him how to hunt for it, but washing it was Rowdy's own idea.

Harriman's ma said Harriman ought to take lessons from Rowdy, because she was sick and tired of always having to tell him to wash up—and use soap while he was at it—when he came in the house after fooling with that coon.

When Harriman got a job stacking feed and sacking groceries at Alford Mercantile after school, Cephus quit waiting in the afternoons by the cattleguard. He just stayed in the house under Granny Ryder's feet till she swatted at him with the whisk broom and told him to quit peskering.

That was when Cephus would go in one of the bedrooms to meddle. He'd pull open the dresser drawers and pick through the old photographs and scarves and envelopes and letters. Cephus had been through all the drawers in all of the bedrooms. He knew what was in all of them. He'd seen pictures of his uncles and his Aunt Rachel in front of the Cedar schoolhouse when they were just children. He'd seen a picture of his mother sitting on a swing. Every time he meddled in Granny Ryder's dresser drawers, he saw the same things. Still, it seemed like he had to do it, like there might be some secret in one of those drawers one time that might tell him something, so in the afternoons Cephus Sumpter would meddle.

At night, he went to bed crying.

He didn't cry loud, Granny Ryder didn't know, but somehow he almost always wound up with his eyes wide open in the dark and his face wet and his chest jouncing when he tried to hold in the hiccups.

And when Cephus finally went to sleep at night, he dreamed.

One gray afternoon when Granny Ryder didn't get up and go to the back bedroom for her nap but fell asleep in her chair with her teeth slipping loose in her mouth so the top ones peeked through her lips like one long sleeping grin, Cephus got up from the floor and put his shoes on and went quietly out the back door.

The air looked like smoke. Cephus stood in the yard (and the chickens weren't out anywhere, were maybe asleep in their house with their heads tucked under their arms because the day was so gray) and looked down the long hill to where the mist swirled up whitish-gray from the ditch under the cattleguard. He couldn't see beyond the ditch to Harriman's house, couldn't even see the road. Cephus started down the hill. The air opened up in front of him and closed behind him so that by the time he reached the cattleguard he could see across the road to the guard on the other side, but he couldn't see Harriman's house, and when he turned and looked behind him, Granny Ryder's house was swallowed up in the gray.

Cephus got scared then.

He took a few steps up the two-lane track until he could see the light from Granny Ryder's front window. He couldn't see the outline of the house but he could see that yellow light like a halo and he knew it was from the floor lamp standing next to Granny's chair. That was fine then, because the house hadn't disappeared and she was still asleep sitting up with her teeth loose in her mouth. That was fine. Cephus turned and went back to the cattle-guard and stared across the road.

After a long time he saw the lights from the school bus coming like two giant steady white eyes at the bottom and two small yellow blinking eyes at the top. The yellow blinking eyes turned red, and the bus stopped in the road. In a bit the blinking red eyes turned back to yellow and the bus grumbled away. Cephus saw the tall talking figures of the Slakemans moving through the grayness up the hill. Harriman hadn't come home on the school bus, Cephus knew that. He knew Harriman never came home that way anymore, knew Harriman's pa brought him home in the pickup after supper, knew Harriman ate a cold supper and did his schoolwork and went to bed. But Cephus had thought maybe today would be different, because of his dream.

He'd waked up from the dream in the morning, waked up crying the same way he'd gone to sleep. His dream told him that Harriman came home on the school bus, like he used to. Harriman climbed the hill, the long high hill from the cattleguard to his house, which seemed in the dream to be longer and higher than ever, and went around back to the porch. He called for Rowdy with the *sssssst-sssst* sound he always made, and Rowdy never came. When Harriman pulled the grate away from the mouth of the rain barrel, the barrel was empty. And when he

looked, he saw Rowdy floating dead in his water pan with his
black eyes open and staring and his little black hands clutched
into fists.

Harriman started crying then, hiccups shuddering and shaking
his chest—except Harriman turned into Cephus crying. Because
Cephus was Harriman and he was the one who never fed Rowdy
or let him hunt in his pockets or played with him anymore. Cephus was the one who killed Rowdy.

But when he looked, Rowdy had waked up from his deadness,
only now he wasn't Rowdy but a chicken hawk with claws and
a sharp beak, and he tumped over the water pan when he flapped
his great slapping wings and flew away.

Cephus tried to see through the grayness to Harriman's house
on the other side of the road, but the air was too thick. He looked
at the mist seeping and swirling upward from the black places
between the cattleguard slats. He thought about Rowdy floating
dead in his water pan. He thought about Harriman coming home
and finding Rowdy. He saw Harriman crying. Cephus's chest
gave up a little heave.

It came clear to him then what he had to do.

He had to go across the road himself to Harriman's house. He
had to go around back to the porch and pick Rowdy up out of
his water pan and carry him out to the cleared place behind the
old tumbledown outhouse. He had to get a shovel out of the barn
and dig a hole in the dirt and bury him, same as Harriman had
done with his redbone pup that ran out in the road and got run
over one time.

Cephus edged closer to the cattleguard.

The memory of the hawk in the dream flapped silently around
him, now coming at him to scratch its claws in his hair, now
lifting, flapping, soaring away. But that hawk was not Rowdy,
and Rowdy was not that hawk. Cephus told himself that.

His feet took him to the first board in the cattleguard. It was
long and flat and dry-boned and splintered. Cephus could see

where it was nailed down in two places on the square beams laid crossways over the ditch. There was a gap between the first slat and the next one, between the next slat and the next, so the cows wouldn't try to cross over. Cows weren't nearly so smart as coons. They thought if they tried to walk over a cattleguard, their hooves would slip right through those gaps and they'd be stuck there forever. They thought the boogers would get them or else they'd break all their legs.

Cephus squatted in the damp dirt and tried to peer through the cracks. It was all darkness or white mist. Boogers lived down there. Cephus didn't know what boogers looked like. Like billy goats maybe, or niggers. Banshees were women and flew in the air at night and screamed. Ghosts were white and you could see all the way through them. They were dead people come back to get something they forgot to take with them when they first died. But boogers were different, and they might eat you if they caught you. They might gnaw your bones with their teeth. Cephus shuddered and stood up and backed away from the ditch.

But then the dream came on him again, and he could see Rowdy floating dead in his water pan. What Cephus knew was, he had to go over there. He had to get that dead coon and take him out back and bury him. He had to show Harriman something.

Cephus took a step forward, and another one. Then he stepped with both feet onto the plank.

The crack seemed to break open and stretch wider in front of him. Cephus stood perfectly still. Boogers couldn't get you as long as you stayed on the cattleguard. They only grabbed you and pulled you down there if your foot slipped though the crack. But that next board was such a dreadful dark distance away. He thought he might jump it with both feet. No sir. That was crazy. What if he slipped? What if he jumped too far and landed with both feet in the next crack and the boogers reached up with their black fingers and *got* him!—just like that. To crunch down on his bones with their terrible white teeth. But Rowdy was floating dead in his water pan and had to be buried. Cephus looked down at his brown shoes on the splintery board.

I'm goin show him, he said to himself. I'm goin show him. Goin show him. He said it out loud.

Cephus's foot lifted in the air and stepped over the crack and came down on the next board. His other foot matched the first one, and then he was standing on the heart of the cattleguard and there was nothing for it but to just keep on going. I'm goin show him, he said.

Cephus stood in the road kicking pebbles. In front of him, behind him, all around him was grayness. Granny Ryder's house was lost in the smoky mist behind him. Harriman's house was not even an outline on the high hill in front. But Cephus felt light in his body, like he might fly right over Harriman's cattleguard if he wanted. He walked across the road and hardly even stopped for a breath before he stepped, one step, two steps, it was only that easy, over Harriman's cattleguard and started climbing the hill.

The light was on in the kitchen. Cephus saw it when he came around to the back of the house. Rowdy's barrel was laying on its side at the corner of the porch, just like always. The three pans were lined up in front of it like they ought to be, but Cephus couldn't see inside them until he climbed up the steps. He used both hands on the railing. His heart beat fierce in his chest. Harriman's ma was running water in the kitchen. Cephus could hear the gushing sound of it inside the kitchen, and the slow drowning gurgle as it sank down the pipe drains under the house.

He stood on the top porch step and stared at the water pans. All three of them were empty. Rowdy wasn't laying there dead and floating. Rowdy wasn't anywhere on the porch to be seen. Then Cephus heard a little scratching sound, and he knew Rowdy was inside his barrel, alive and living, scratching his little fingers on the sloping wooden slats. Cephus took a step forward. Rowdy stood up on his hind paws and grabbed hold of the icebox grate. He stared at Cephus with his shining black eyes wrapped in their dark mask.

Cephus felt his heart squeeze tight and then let go in one long aching breath. Rowdy wasn't dead. Rowdy wasn't a chicken hawk. Cephus's dream had been lying to him. Rowdy was just Rowdy, inside his home.

"Ssssst-sssst," Cephus said. "Here, boy." Cephus went over to the rain barrel and bent down, grunting and pushing, to shove the concrete blocks out of the way. He kicked the grate with his shoe and it fell off to the side.

Rowdy stayed inside the barrel, looking out at Cephus.

"Ssssst-sssst," Cephus said.

Rowdy watched him from the mouth of the rain barrel, his eyes glinting black sparks in the gray smoky light.

"I thought you was dead," Cephus said. "I come over here to bury you."

Still, Rowdy watched him.

"I had me this dream," Cephus said.

Rowdy turned around and went back into the dark reaches of the rain barrel. Cephus started crying then. He kicked the side of the rain barrel and said a few cuss words. Harriman's ma was still running water in the kitchen. Cephus went over and sat down on the edge of the porch. "I hate that damn coon," he said to himself, crying.

When he heard Rowdy's fingernails clicking on the porch floor, Cephus turned and looked. Rowdy came waddling toward him, the harsh gray hair on his belly sticking out in all directions, the black rings on his tail dragging limp along the wood. It seemed like Cephus could see Rowdy when he was a bitty baby, how his baby hands held things, how his small face slid down to a point at his shiny black nose. Rowdy's hair had been soft then, not stiff like a hairbrush. Cephus's chest just would not be still.

Rowdy came up beside him and stuck his nose close to Ce-

phus's arm. Cephus could hear Rowdy's nose snuffling. Then
Rowdy stood on his hind paws and raised his head up over Cephus's shoulder. Rowdy's hind paws were like his front paws only
longer, four black fingers with silver claws and a thumb. Rowdy
balanced on the narrow black pads of his hind paws and started
hunting through Cephus's front shirt pocket. Cephus sat very
still.

"I didn't bring anything to feed you, boy," Cephus whispered.
"I thought you was dead."

Cephus considered about going to the back door and asking
Harriman's ma for some lettuce leaves, but Rowdy was holding
onto his shoulder, the claws on the coon's fingers digging through
his shirt right into his skin.

"Hey," Cephus said. "Here, now. You quit that."

But Rowdy wouldn't quit it. He danced around Cephus's back
on his hind paws, holding on to Cephus, his claws like silver
needles scratching into his back.

"Quit it!" Cephus shouted, and tried to get up. But Rowdy
pulled him over backwards and started clawing his head.

Cephus tried to holler for Harriman's ma, but it was like a
dream where you shout but no sound will come out of you. Rowdy
held onto him. The fingers picked through his scalp, gouging
and scratching, clawing the flesh. Cephus was screaming for real
now, long, thin, high screams that seemed like they came from
up high near the porch roof, but Harriman's ma was running the
water and she never came. Cephus hated her. He hated Harriman. Rowdy's claws were like fire raining down on his head.

1967

Lyla Mae Muncy met Jack Allen on the next-to-the-last day of Falls Creek Baptist Assembly Summer Bible Church Camp, and if it hadn't been for the fact that she hadn't had one single boyfriend the whole entire week (while her best friend Verna Wadley was sitting with a new boy at practically every service), she probably wouldn't have paid any attention to him even then. In the first place he wasn't all that tall and his eyes were a little strange and staring and besides Lyla Mae thought he might be weird because it seemed like he liked her *too* much. But on the other hand he was kind of cute (Verna said so) and those eyes that stared so strangely out from beneath his black brows were a very interesting shade of green, pale in the center and outlined with turquoise, so that they seemed to light up his dark face. And after all he was *there*, following her down the hill from her cabin to the refreshment stand and the Baptist Book Store, and then back up the hill, sitting outside in the dust while she ate lunch.

After a while it became almost easy for Lyla Mae to ignore the awkward way Jack Allen stood with his head tipped forward and his hands never knowing what to do. She ignored, too, the creeping sensation on the back of her neck every time he looked up from beneath his black brows and grinned his slow grin and drawled, "I sure wisht we didn't have to go home tomorrow, don't you?" (which he must have said ten times if he said it once on that long afternoon). And the truth is, Lyla Mae had just turned fifteen, which, even in those days, was time enough for a girl to find out a thing or two about boys. So after Jack Allen had followed her around the whole afternoon and got her to promise to sit with him during the final evening worship service and walked her back to her cabin afterwards, shyly holding on to her sweaty hand in the dark, Lyla Mae Muncy thought she might be in love.

They said goodbye the next day after lunch. Lyla Mae climbed on board the Bartlesville First Baptist bus and hurried to the back, where she made Verna Wadley scoot out of the way so she could wave her hands out the window and watch Jack Allen grow smaller as the bus pulled away. She liked to imagine, during the long depressing trip home, that she'd seen tears glistening at the edges of Jack Allen's green eyes.

All that was fine, and Lyla had a very successful time of it telling her friends back home about this Jack Allen she met at summer camp (and he got taller and cuter and his eyes got greener every time she told it), but the one thing she hadn't counted on was how close Bartlesville was to the town of Ramona, where Jack Allen lived. A month to the day after Falls Creek was over, he called her up, long-distance, and asked her if she'd like to go out on a date.

Lyla Mae was quiet for a long time on the phone (with Jack Allen saying, "Lyla? Lyla? Lyla?" in her ear) because she couldn't get over the feeling that one of her daydreams had called her up on the telephone and it might just as well have been Paul McCartney on the other end of the line as Jack Allen. Finally, though, she realized that this was an actual long-distance phone call, which Jack Allen's parents were probably having to pay for, and she'd better say something. She whispered, "I'll have to go ask my mother."

Lyla stood in front of her mother with her fingers twisted together behind her back and one sandaled foot standing on top of the other one, mumbling the words. And Lyla's mother said yes.

Lyla Mae stared at her mother in wonder. Didn't she realize that Ramona was a town nineteen miles away down Highway 75? Didn't she realize that Lyla hardly *knew* this boy? Didn't she realize that Jack Allen probably didn't even have a driver's license and the whole thing was going to be totally illegal? Worse yet, didn't she realize that her daughter Lyla Mae had never been out on an actual honest-to-goodness car date before in her life and wouldn't have the faintest idea how to act? But Lyla's mother said yes. She didn't even have to think about it very long, she just lifted her head from her ironing and stared at Lyla Mae for the briefest moment with her teeth locked over her bottom lip, and then said, "I don't see why not." Just like that.

Lyla went back to the phone. "My mom says okay," she said, her voice coming out of a dream. Then she added quickly, "But I gotta be home early. Like about . . . nine o'clock." Jack Allen said okay, he would pick her up at five-thirty Saturday night. Lyla Mae hung up the phone, whispering to herself, "*Five-thirty? In the afternoon?*"

Well, the week wore on and Lyla Mae spent a great many hours in her parents' bedroom with the door closed, talking on the extension to Verna Wadley and the others about this upcoming date with Jack Allen. She carefully squeezed every drop of excitement out of each conversation (and after all, wasn't he driving nearly forty miles round trip to come pick her up?), so that by the time she hung up she'd be flushed a soft pink (or so the mirror above her mom's dresser told her) and her heart would be pounding, and she'd have a clear, brave image of Jack Allen standing in the sunlight with one foot hiked up on the fender of his convertible car.

But when she sat alone in the bathtub at night with her transistor radio propped on the ledge and her hair stuffed up inside a shower cap, Lyla Mae worried. What if he turned out to be a creep? What if, when she actually saw him, he turned out to be actually even shorter than she remembered? What if (and this is the thought that scared her the most every time she thought it)—what if he tried to kiss her? Lyla shuddered every time she came to that part and turned the radio up louder and sang along with The Mamas and The Papas until her brother banged on the bathroom door and yelled at her to shut up she was waking the dead. And so the nights of the week wore on, and before Lyla Mae could stop it, Saturday came.

Lyla went through her closet and all her drawers a total of seven times before she finally made up her mind what to wear, and then her daddy made her march right back to the bedroom and change clothes at four-thirty because he said no daughter of his was going out on a date in no pair of *shorts,* and Lyla said, Daddy, they're not shorts, they're *culottes,* for heaven's sake, but her daddy just looked at her and Lyla went to her bedroom and changed into a skirt.

She came back to the living room and sat on the couch and stared at the television, which wasn't even on, and pressed her lips together so hard the lipstick made a caked smudge all along the outside curve of her mouth. The clock on the wall above the television pushed relentlessly on toward five-thirty. When the long minute hand had just nearly reached the six, a car horn blared in the driveway and then a knock came rap-rap-a-rap-rap . . . rap-rap! on the storm door. Lyla could see the white of his shirt sleeve through the screen.

Lyla's daddy said from behind his newspaper, "Answer the door, Lyla Mae." It's a good thing Lyla's mother happened to be coming around the corner from the kitchen just at that moment because Lyla's rear end was definitely glued to the couch.

Lyla's mother pushed the screen open, and Jack Allen stepped inside. Lyla's daddy shook out his newspaper, got up from his chair, and held out his hand to Jack Allen, saying, "How do you do, my boy? How do you do?" And for the first time Lyla realized that her daddy wasn't any more practiced at this than she was.

Jack Allen said, "How do you do, Mr. Muncy?" And then he said, "How do you do, Mrs. Muncy?" and Lyla's mother said, "Fine."

Lyla Mae took a deep breath and looked up at Jack Allen.

Well, he didn't look too bad. His eyes were still strange and staring and the shape of his head was a lot rounder than she'd remembered (which the haircut he'd gotten since Falls Creek didn't help much), but on the other hand he hadn't shrunk any, and if he wasn't any taller than her, at least he wasn't shorter. His hands didn't seem any more comfortable, dangling there at the ends of his arms, but when he grinned, the white of his shirt seemed to reflect off his teeth and make his skin look darker and more mysterious. And there was, after all, that curious color of his eyes.

Jack Allen grinned at Lyla Mae and said, "You ready?" Lyla Mae heard her brother thumping down the hall toward the living room in Daddy's old fishing waders, which he'd taken to wearing at every conceivable opportunity. She stood up and breathed a quick "Yes," and brushed past Jack Allen to push open the storm door. At the last minute she remembered to wave goodbye to her parents over Jack Allen's white shoulder and called out, much too loudly, so that half the neighborhood must have heard, "Don't worry, Mom, I'll be home early." Then Lyla Mae turned around and saw what was waiting for her in the driveway. In broad daylight. For all the world to see.

In Lyla Mae's driveway sat a shabby red pickup with the faded white letters LEO'S PLUMBING AND HEATING * EMERGENCY SERVICE * ANY DAY * ANY HOUR * NO JOB TOO SMALL inscribed on the door. Behind the wheel of the shabby red pickup sat the fattest man Lyla Mae had ever seen in her life, and beside the fat man sat a thin woman with brown lanky hair and squinting brown eyes and a large gap in the front of her face where a tooth should have been. Lyla Mae stood very still and felt her blood draining down to her toes. It wasn't just that she wanted the concrete of the driveway to open up and swallow her whole. It wasn't even the horrible clash between the red convertible she'd imagined and this monstrosity piece of junk sitting plunked in her driveway. It was the fact that she couldn't believe that anybody—*anybody*—who liked and respected a girl and wanted to impress her on the first date would show up in a contraption such as that with a crew of people such as those.

Numbly, she followed Jack Allen across the driveway. Jack said, "That's my uncle. Leo. And Nettie's his girl." Then Lyla Mae understood. Of course. Jack Allen wasn't old enough to drive a car, she knew that already. *Somebody* had to drive them around and let them off at the show (naturally they were going to a movie because that's the only place in Bartlesville anyone ever went for a date) and then pick them up later and bring Lyla Mae home. Lyla gazed ahead at Jack Allen's hunched shoulders with a look of grave sympathy. She knew how it was. She had relatives too.

Jack opened the door for her and stepped back to let her climb in. Lyla Mae got an awkward grip on the door handle and an even more awkward grip on the glove box and somehow managed to get into the truck. Jack swung himself in after her and slammed the old clanging door loud enough to wake the dead, not to mention Mrs. Engstrand's new baby across the street.

Leo said, "Hi there, sugar," and Nettie squinted her eyes, and Jack Allen said, "Lyla, meet Leo. And this here is Nettie." Lyla stared straight ahead through the dirty windshield (but not before she caught a glimpse of that man Leo *winking* at her, of all things!) and said, "Pleased to meet you, I'm sure." She cut her eyes over at Jack then, but he just grinned at her. He didn't seem the least bit embarrassed over the size or manners of his Uncle Leo. He seemed to think conditions were perfectly normal. Lyla stared at the windshield again. Leo started the truck with a cough and a sputter, backed it out of the drive, and the four of them, packed into one seat like a can of sardines, drove away down the street.

The pickup chugged through the town (with Lyla Mae shrinking down in the seat, staring at her crossed fingers in her lap and praying that nobody who knew her was out on the streets of Bartlesville at five-thirty on this Saturday afternoon) and headed

across the long bridge over the Caney River to the east side of
town, where the new shopping mall sprawled with its double
cinema and J. C. Penney's and spanking new Rec Hall. But Leo
didn't turn into the parking lot of Eastland Mall. He turned south
on Highway 75.

Lyla Mae sat up straight. Well, we *can't* be going to the Hilltop
Drive-In Theater, she thought, because it's still stark daylight
outside (and it's a good thing too, she thought, because drive-in
movies are definitely risky business on a first date—or on any
date, for that matter—everybody knows that), and we can't be
going to the Green Country Inn to eat dinner because anybody
in their right mind could see these guys can't afford that place,
and it's a cinch we're not headed to the only other single public
structure out this way, which is Limestone Elementary School.

Lyla Mae looked over at Jack. He had somehow managed to
unwedge his arm from where it had been trapped between them
and now had it draped across the back of the seat. Very casual.
Lyla shrank a little to her left, so as to not give Jack Allen any
ideas, and jabbed herself on Nettie's sharp elbow. She pulled
herself up straight and stared straight ahead and listened to Jack
and his uncle yell at each other over the roar of the motor about
plumbing and crops and the St. Louis Cardinals.

South on Highway 75 they went, past Green Country Inn and
the Hilltop and Limestone Elementary School, past the shingled
ranch-style houses on the edge of Bartlesville city limits, past the
sign that said TULSA, 50 MI., and on and on south. Towards
Ramona.

Lyla Mae wracked her memory. Had he told her they were
going to Ramona when he called her up and asked her for a date?
Had he mentioned anything at all about where they were going
and who they were going with and what they would do when
they got there and all those other details which Lyla's mother, if
she was any kind of decent, concerned mother at all, surely
should have *asked* Lyla about? But Lyla's memory of Jack Allen's

phone call was as vague as a month-old daydream. Perfectly worthless. And Jack Allen and his uncle continued to yell at each other over the roar of the motor, and Nettie's sharp elbow continued to poke her in the side, and the wind thundered through the open windows and whipped Lyla's hair, which she'd spent an hour and a half combing and spraying, into a tangled stiff mess, and Lyla Mae was starting to sweat.

Three times Lyla opened her mouth to ask Jack Allen about where they were going, and three times the howl of the wind and the motor and the uncomfortable notion that probably he had told her but she just hadn't listened made her clamp her lips back tightly together and twist her hands in her lap and tell herself, wait, just wait. Then she said, God, if you get me out of this, I promise I'll start listening from now on and quit bragging whenever I can help it and never take a drink as long as I live and I know I helped drink that two ounces of whiskey Sharon Frakes smuggled into math class last spring but that was just an experiment and I promise I never will again.

The sun was beginning to lower itself toward the horizon by the time Leo slowed the truck to turn off the highway. Lyla Mae uncorked her stiff neck and turned to gaze up at the great squared-off white house that sat high on a hill overlooking the town. That house was Lyla Mae's only association with the town of Ramona. If anybody ever said the word "Ramona" (including that afternoon at Falls Creek when Jack Allen told her where he was from), the first picture that jumped into her mind was that white house, huge and lonesome, high on the hill. You could see it for miles from either direction along Highway 75. It stood like a lighthouse or beacon, and Lyla Mae had long held the notion that the house signaled some special secret about the town.

She stared at it now as they passed below. The lowering sun glinted off the windows, turning the glass to gold and fire, and Lyla scrunched down in the seat to watch it, thinking how it was almost like a great mansion, one that belonged to some other time, some other state somewhere deep in the South. She glanced sideways at Jack Allen, trying to fit his dark face and green eyes to the idea of a mansion, but when he felt her watching him and turned his staring eyes to look back at her, Lyla looked quickly away. She leaned forward and held her breath, a vague skittery excitement rising inside her, as the pickup nosed off the highway.

Lyla Mae had never seen Ramona. She'd ridden past it a thousand times on the way down to Cedar to visit Nana and Grandpa, on the way to Tulsa, on the way to anyplace really, because practically the only way out of Bartlesville was south on 75, but Ramona itself sat just off the highway, hidden by the folding curves of hills, and Lyla Mae had never seen it. Leo coaxed the coughing truck around a bend, and the white house disappeared.

They humped and puffed and chugged along main street. Lyla sat back to look at the buildings rolling slowly past the truck's dirty windows and felt her brief burst of excitement fading away. Ramona didn't look much different from Cedar. It didn't, in fact, look any different from any Okie small town Lyla Mae had ever seen: a few flat storefronts, a gas station, the usual old Tastee-Freez, and of course, the pool hall, where two men leaned back against the smoky windows and lifted a forefinger lazily in the warm air as Leo honked. Lyla scanned the street for a sign of a movie theater, but she couldn't see one. Main Street looked closed down and empty, and Leo drove on.

Leo pushed the old pickup on through the town, past the white clapboard houses with their porches deep in shadow, past Ramona First Baptist with its pitifully thin steeple and the Assembly of God that looked more like a parsonage with sad-eyed dark windows than a church. On through Ramona to the outskirts of town where Leo nosed the truck over a low-lying ditch onto a trampled and dusty parking area where cars and pickups and farm trucks were parked helter-skelter, this way and that, in no perceptible pattern, as far as Lyla Mae's narrowed eyes could see. Leo allowed the pickup's engine to die, as it had been trying valiantly to do since it left Lyla Mae's driveway, and pulled the emergency brake toward him with a grunt and a grating screech and a massive heave of his shoulders that sent shock waves rippling through the front seat.

Jack shoved on the door handle and jumped out. He grinned up at Lyla Mae and offered his hand. Lyla stared down at Jack Allen standing in the dust with his round head tipped forward and his green eyes staring and his awkward hand lifted toward her. Shakily she held out her hand, and Jack Allen helped Lyla get down from the truck. Nettie clambered out behind her, and together the three of them walked around to the other side where Leo was using both arms—one braced on the steering wheel, the other against the back of the seat—and both legs, planted firmly on the floorboard but pointed toward the open door, and a great number of grunts to hoist himself out of the truck.

When Leo stood, finally, on the dusty lot, Lyla Mae glanced up at his face. His head was tucked forward and his ears and neck were a burnt shade of red. His massive shoulders heaved beneath the dense blue cotton of his shirt. As Lyla Mae watched, the burnt red color crept up from his neck to cover his face. Leo grinned at her (with a grin so like Jack Allen's she shivered inside and thought to herself, and what if I was to *marry* him and when he grew up and got old he was going to look like *that!*) and said, "You hungry, shug? You want a hot dog or something? Jackie, don't just stand there like a bump on a log, where's your manners, go get this young lady a hot dog."

Jack Allen said, "Lyla? You want a hot dog?"

Lyla shook her head no and turned around, perplexed, and began to walk toward the most crowded, haphazard row of pick-ups and cars. Jack Allen caught up to her and touched her elbow and began to guide her gently, barely brushing her elbow with his warm hand, between the cars to the open space beyond.

Lyla Mae stopped. And stared. And felt her heart sinking down to rest on the tops of her new white leather sandals. Before her,

bathed in the yellowish glow of a late summer evening and crisscrossed with long grotesquely black shadows and pulsating
greener than the greenest emerald she'd ever imagined, lay a ball
field.

A *ball* game? she said to herself. You mean to tell me on the
first date ever in my whole entire life he brings me to the town
of Ramona to a *baseball* game? Lyla Mae thought maybe she
really and truly wanted to die.

She looked around her, at the rickety bleachers packed with
country people (and Lyla Mae knew for a fact they were all country people, because there's a certain look about the ones that
come in from the country, a sort of dusty, stringy-haired look that
blends the color of their skins and eyes and hair into one snuff-
colored shade of drab); she looked at the players warming up on
the field in their makeshift uniforms and bright new caps, at the
barefooted kids chasing each other and screaming underneath
the bleachers, at the deceitful sun sinking toward the horizon in
a fiery ball. I don't believe this, Lyla Mae said to herself. Jack
Allen touched her elbow again and Lyla did not even turn to look
but just made her way in a trance to the nearest row of bleachers.

They climbed nearly to the top and Lyla Mae sat down next to
a fat woman holding a bawling baby in her arms, and then was
shocked when the fat woman turned to her and smiled. She
wasn't a woman at all but a girl not much older than Lyla Mae,
dressed in the clothes and weariness and attitude of a woman.
Lyla quickly turned her eyes to the playing field.

Well. Those weren't even boys out there tossing that ball
around and swinging those arms full of bats. They were full-
grown adult men. Lyla had been to ball games before (not to
watch the game, of course, but to see who was there and let them
see her and spend a lot of time going back and forth to the
concession stand), but it had always been Little League or else
at the school. She'd never seen such a thing as these full-grown
adult men parading around so serious on the field in their red

caps and orange caps and mishmash uniforms. She watched them with her mouth half open. It seemed like the world or else the town of Ramona was upside down and backwards, because here she was sitting next to a girl who carried herself like a woman, and down there on the field were all these grown men doing things exactly like boys.

Jack leaned in close to her ear and asked her if she wanted a Coke. Lyla Mae shook her head. She could feel him shifting on the splintery bench, and from the downcast corner of her eyes saw his dirty sneakers crossing and uncrossing themselves. His right hand pressed against the side of her skirt and she knew good and well he wanted her to unclasp her own hands from where they lay knotted in her lap and let one of them slip into his. Baloney. Lyla Mae eased herself closer to the fat woman and let her knotted hands stay just politely where they were.

Men in orange caps ran out onto the field while the people all around her whistled and stamped their feet till Lyla thought the whole stand of bleachers might cave in at any minute. She looked down to see Leo and Nettie at the foot of the bleachers, and as she watched they began to make their way toward the top. Lyla Mae did not want to stare but she just could not help herself.

Leo came first, lumbering like a bull elephant and grunting and wheezing so frightfully Lyla felt her own chest tighten in pain. Why oh why, if he was ever going to let himself get in that shape in the first place, why didn't he have the decency to stay at home in a darkened room instead of parading his enormous self out in public for all the world to have to see? And why (now this is the element that Lyla really couldn't understand), why was that poor scrawny little Nettie even with him in the first place? She wasn't *that* homely, not if she kept her mouth shut so you couldn't see the gap where a tooth should have been. But here she came, silent as a spirit behind him, with one hand held up toward his back but never quite touching, as if, should he actually start to fall, she could really do something to stop him.

And the amazing thing was, nobody seemed to be taking any notice. Not that they didn't notice Leo, because most of the men greeted him, and the women too, murmuring, "Hey, Leo," and "Evening, Mr. Allen," and "Nice night for it, ain't it?," but nobody seemed to find his laborious ascent painful or disturbing or anything out of the ordinary. They acted just casual, that's all, as if they'd seen him climb those steps or any other steps in the town of Ramona a hundred times in their lives and the way Leo Allen climbed them was no different from the way any other body might. Lyla finally remembered her manners. She turned her eyes away just as Leo arrived at the end of their seat.

Jack squeezed against her to make more room and Lyla in turn had to crowd up even closer against the fat woman, and then the board beneath her rear end groaned and dipped as Leo sat down, and Lyla thought to herself, well, here I am, out on my first date ever in my whole entire life, surrounded by all these *fat* people. And she thought, this is what I am never, ever going to do. I am never going to end up a fat woman at a ball game on a Saturday night. Never.

Lyla pulled her right arm in close to her side and tried to shrink away from the fat woman, as if fatness and crying babies and getting old before your time were diseases that could rub off on a person. She held her left arm stiff against her body, retreating from the warmth of Jack Allen's shoulder, and in this position, with her hands clamped together and her knees locked tight and her shoulders hiked up about halfway to her ears, Lyla Mae turned her eyes on the ball game. She pretended to watch and pretended to be interested, not that she liked baseball or even understood it, any more than she understood football, though she knew baseball was a simpler game because the language of it was more or less plain English instead of sacks and offsides and first-down-and-ten. She thought if she kept her eyes on the field and didn't ask any questions and nodded her head in all the right places then hopefully Jack Allen wouldn't feel it his duty to ex-

plain it to her. She didn't really feel like listening to Jack Allen
explain the game of baseball.

The crowd of country people never once let up with its hooting
and hollering, though Lyla Mae could not figure out what was
so exciting because they yelled if the players just stood around
gawking at each other the same as when somebody was running
around the bases. She glanced over at Jack Allen. He was sitting
all hunched forward in his seat with his lips parted and his green
eyes staring and glinting in the twilight. But his right hand was
still at his side, captured between them, cupped open, waiting.
Lyla Mae squeezed her hands tighter together in her lap and
thanked her lucky stars that she'd already made it a point to
mention that she had to be home *early*. She thought that maybe
when half-time came it wouldn't be too rude to remind Jack Allen
of that fact. What in the world was she going to tell everyone
when they asked her what she did on her date?

Lyla skipped her eyes past Jack Allen to the silent, squint-eyed
Nettie, and then past her to Leo, huge and sweating, hollering
in his rolling voice to kill the ump. The yellow floodlights on their
tall poles were picking up details in the oncoming dark. She could
see the way the sweat ran in rivulets between the folds of Leo's
neck. She could see the white scalp under Jack Allen's too-short
haircut. A tight feeling pushed in on Lyla, squeezing her chest
till she thought she couldn't breathe.

All they ever talk about, she thought, is ball games and plumbing. That's all they ever talk about in their whole lives, I bet.

Lyla clenched her hands against the front of her chest. She
looked back toward the field, where men in red caps stood around
with their big gloves dangling in a mauve-colored haze. She tried
to think about the hard shiny surfaces at the high school where
she would be going in a few weeks, the clean lines, bright colors,
all that glistening chrome in the basement cafeteria. She wanted
to imagine herself and Verna Wadley standing in line in crisp
new school clothes, joking with the others, tossing their hair. But

Lyla couldn't concentrate on her pictures of high school, because it was in that moment that Jack Allen made his move. Lyla's hands were still locked together in front of her, but that didn't deter old Jack Allen, he just reached around behind her back and wrapped his fingers around her waist. Lyla jumped and swung her head to stare at him. Jack Allen never took his eyes off the game. But she could see how his head was tipped forward and his face was starting to turn the same dusky red as his uncle's.

The solid *whack!* of hard wood slapping leather silenced all other sound. Lyla felt the echoes of it slide in her ears and down the back of her throat. Then the crowd came to its feet like one single being, shouting, Go! Go! Go! Go!, and the bleachers quaked with the rocking and pounding and thundering of feet. The fat woman hoisted her baby in the air. Nettie jumped up, and even Leo gathered himself and pushed off from the bleachers and finally stood at the end of the bench. The crowd's wave of excitement pushed through Lyla, trying to lift her, but Jack Allen stayed where he was, with his warm palm pressing lightly against Lyla Mae's waist. She moved to get up, but Jack's hand seemed like a weight, though he only touched her lightly. Lyla's shoulders went rigid, her spine locked tight, teeth clamped together. The old creeping sensation returned to crawl up the back of her neck like a memory. But she let Jack Allen pull her toward him.

They sat that way while the crowd settled back down, laughing and restless. Children pushed past them, stepping on Lyla's feet as they rushed to the concession stand. Jack Allen kept his hand just there. He didn't pull her tight, still touched her only lightly, his fingers moving in a soft kneading motion against the cotton, the heat of his skin seeping through her blouse. She relaxed a little against him. She felt his chest move up and down with his breathing. She could feel the slim, hard bones there, and his heart, thudding in a fierce rhythm against her back. Lyla turned her face toward him. A clean, warm soap smell radiated from his shirt collar, the side of his neck. Lyla felt her shoulder blades soften. She shifted on the bench, leaning against Jack Allen, settling in.

The sounds of the crowd and the ball game drifted away. Lyla closed her eyes on the faces and shoulders and tops of the heads of the country people, felt the rhythm of her breath slow to match Jack Allen's breathing. She thought about Verna Wadley, about what she might like to tell Verna Wadley.

Shouts and a wave of loud laughter rose from the crowd. Sleepily, Lyla opened her eyes. She looked up at the rusted scoreboard. It said HOME 4 . . . VISITORS 13. She looked down at the field. Men's faces floated like moons under the floodlights, orange caps phosphorescent in the purple-tinged air. Lyla looked over at the fat woman, who now held a Coke cup in one puffy fist and a baby bottle in the other, both containers lifted in the air like pom-poms or medals, the baby tiny and sleeping, moving its wet tiny mouth, in her lap. On the far side of the fat woman stretched the long row of country people, all of them dull-looking and drab in their clothes, but shifting and moving, shaking their fists and laughing and yelling.

Lyla Mae sat very still. She watched a man in blue overalls stand up and put two fingers in his mouth to whistle. He had no teeth in his mouth. Not one. His gums mashed together like flattened inner tubes. And he wasn't an old man either, he couldn't have been any older than Lyla Mae's daddy, with his brown hair slicked back over his ears and laid down with grease, with his hard-muscled arms waving in the air. Lyla looked past him to the woman beside him. Her hair lay in little close ringlets like doggy turds all over her head. Her plump knees spread themselves wide under her skirt. She was fat too, like so many of the women, her skin rippling in soft folds along the side of her cheek. She was smiling and clapping her hands. Beyond her, another man and another woman rocked back and forth, hollering, their snuff-colored faces split wide with laughter (and Lyla thought to herself, what in the world are they *laughing* for, I mean, aren't they *losing?*) and beyond them, other cheering men and women, and kids, wiggling on the bench, flashing their big asking eyes, jabbing the air with their elbows and knees. Lyla watched them. She tried to figure why she should suddenly feel so strange, why turning her eyes down that noisy turbulent row should make her mouth go dry and her heart beat fast and the back of her neck crinkle up with the hairs going the wrong way.

Lyla shook her head. Her breath rushed out in little short gasps. Again she shook it, but already she knew it was no use. There was no way to shake off the feeling that she knew these people. That she'd known them all her life.

It wasn't just the familiar color of their skins and eyes and hair, or the way the women wore their skirts too long and their hair in styles that should have disappeared in the fifties. It wasn't that any man or boy down that long row could have changed places with any one of her daddy's uncles or cousins who still lived at Cedar. Or that her own daddy's hometown—any Okie small town she'd ever been through, in fact—held a population of people exactly like these, lounging in front of the courthouse, sitting in their pickups at the Sonic Drive-In.

It was something different, something cold and troublesome, like watching a person come toward you from the other side of a dark window, and then, when you get close, finding out it wasn't somebody else at all, but just your self coming toward you. Just your own common reflection.

I don't belong here, Lyla Mae said to herself. Here is not where I belong. She thought that by saying, almost praying it, she could guarantee herself the truth and the fact of it. But deep in the most secret reaches of her being, Lyla Mae was afraid.

Jack Allen slid his hand up her back to the top of her shoulder. He draped it around her, casually, publicly, right out there in the open for God or any one of the fat neighbors to see. A sickening knot appeared in Lyla Mae's stomach.

He's acting like it's the most natural thing in the world, she thought. He's acting like I belong here, like I just fit right on in, and the next thing you know he'll be asking me to come over and visit with his parents. Next thing, he'll be expecting me to come to Ramona *every* Saturday night.

She tried to pull herself up straight on the bench, but the pressure of Jack Allen's hand on her shoulder held her down. Lyla felt herself caught still and paralyzed, held in one place by the weight of Jack Allen's hand. She felt it like a judgment. Like being doomed to sit home on Saturday nights for eternity. Like being formed by God in the shape of a country person. Like being sent straight down to hell.

She could be stuck there forever.

In a town like the town of Ramona forever.

With nothing to talk about but ball games and plumbing.

Nothing to hope for but sitting fat in the bleachers and yelling, and opening her pocketbook for dirty-mouthed kids.

Lyla wrenched her shoulder away from Jack Allen and jumped to her feet. "I got to get home!" she said, squeezing her voice out between the clamps that were choking her throat. "When's half-time? What time is it? I got to get home!"

On the silent ride back through the town of Ramona, through the flat empty streets, past the hollow churches and the closed-down pool hall, Lyla Mae talked to herself. It's not my fault if I have to be home early, she said, I told him that first thing on the phone. Can I help it if their stupid old game wasn't over? And she thought, I wonder if I have to count this as my actual first date. I mean, I wonder if I couldn't just count this as a night at a ball game in the town of Ramona and start all over again about dating after school starts in the fall.

As Leo turned the pickup onto the highway, Lyla Mae hunkered down in the seat. She twisted her neck to look up at the white house. The house's windows were dark, but garish light from a tall modern pole in the yard swept over its face, making it look more alone, more secret, more distant and high and farther away. Lyla felt her chest tighten with a strange, awful longing.

I bet that was nobody from *this* town ever lived there, she thought.

But of course it was, sometime. It had to have been.

The pickup squeaked and rattled northward. The lights of Ramona dwindled behind them and disappeared finally, swallowed by the dark rolling turns. Lyla forced the last air out of her lungs. She tried to twist the sinking feeling in her chest into a sigh of relief. At least Bartlesville was no more than nineteen miles away. Her breath came out shaky. At least there was school starting and new clothes to think about, and . . . and maybe getting herself a new haircut or something. At least there was Verna Wadley to call up on the phone the next day. She thought maybe she could tell Verna that Jack Allen lived in that white mansion, you know the one, that huge famous mansion that stands up on that hill, overlooking Ramona. She tried to make up a story to go with the mansion, a story to include her date and Jack Allen's green eyes and a red convertible car. But the clean soap smell of Jack Allen's shirt collar, the rise and fall of his breathing, the final stark glimpse of the house through the pickup's back window, white walls bled by the yard light to a strange, peeling dove color, windows black and empty, all kept hold of her, and no story would come.

Lyla could feel Nettie's slack bones shoving against her, Jack Allen's arm on the back of the seat behind her head. The cool night wind rolled in through the windows. Lyla watched the dark line of hills rolling past them, the sparse sprinkle of stars hanging low in the sky. She sat stiffly, trying to keep herself pulled in and separate from Jack Allen and Nettie, but she was wedged in between them too tightly not to be touched.

1968

Lyla Mae Muncy hated her cousin Nikki for a variety of reasons, not the least of which was the fact that she spelled her name with two *k*'s—an affectation that Lyla Mae found totally unbearable—although Nikki also had big boobs and blond hair and she lived in California, any single factor of which would have probably been sufficient reason to hate her no matter how she spelled her name.

But in Lyla Mae's sixteenth summer, which was also Nikki's sixteenth summer (a coincidence which the family found significant and about which they kept reminding them both on countless stupid occasions: somehow because they were born four days apart they were supposed to be these great friends or something), Nikki was shipped back to Oklahoma. Lyla Mae, too, was packed up with all her summer things in Bartlesville and the two of them were loaded onto a bus at the Trailways station in Tulsa and sent down to Cedar to stay with Nana and Grandpa. The plan was, as nearly as Lyla Mae could figure, for their preacher granddaddy to put the fear of God in them so that Nikki, especially, might mend her evil ways before she wound up on the road to eternal damnation. Or else for Lyla Mae to be a good influence on Nikki and help guide her back on the road to salvation. Or else for them to just stay out of trouble because Cedar was such a boring little town that there wouldn't be anything there for them to get in trouble about.

"I can't belie-e-e-ve this," Nikki said from the back of the Trailways bus, where she was blowing smoke in the direction of the overhead luggage rack. "This has got to be the most unbelievable thing that has ever happened to me in my whole entire life." Nikki was not happy about having to spend her summer "in goddamn godforsaken Podunk with a bunch of goddamn hick Okies." She made certain Lyla Mae understood that.

Lyla watched Nikki's smoke rings float upward, expanding, until they finally broke themselves on Lyla Mae's mother's blond vanity case crammed sideways in the rack. Lyla placed the side of her finger beneath her nostrils and pressed upward. She did this casually, as if lost in contemplation of some deep philosophical question. The stench from the toilet across the aisle mingling with the odor of dozens of old cigarette butts crammed in the ashtrays on the backs of the seats was making her want to puke. Nikki had insisted they sit in the back of the bus. As Lyla Mae watched, Nikki did something very peculiar with her cigarette smoke. Either she was releasing it out of her mouth and sucking it in through her nostrils, or else she was blowing it out through her nostrils and inhaling it into her mouth. Lyla couldn't tell which. In any case, it made a very interesting streaming blanket of smoke which sailed swiftly between Nikki's nose and mouth. It looked very sophisticated.

Lyla Mae turned away to watch the shaggy roadside race by outside the window. Dust-dulled grasses, sumac, scrawny scrub oaks clotted the ditches on both sides of the highway, crowding toward the blacktop. This state always looks like it needs a haircut, she thought. And in spite of herself, there was a pang of shame mixed in with the thought. She never had been able to figure out how it was that Nikki could make her feel so fiercely defensive and at the same time so ashamed of something that had absolutely nothing to do with her or her life—namely, the state that she lived in.

When they were fourteen, Nikki had flown back for Christmas along with her mom (her daddy being long gone out of the picture and nobody ever talked about him), and when she stepped off the plane with her mousy brown hair bleached to a platinum blond and two softly mounded boobs pushing up from her chest like early mushrooms that appear overnight in the spring and her skin tanned to a tawny glaze—in *December*, for pity's sake —she gave Lyla Mae to understand that it was because she lived in California that these things were possible. In their fifteenth summer she changed her name from Nicole May (the four days between their births being, unfortunately, in the month of May, which accounted for the middle names they each unfortunately possessed) to the hateful "Nikki" and wrote Lyla that she had a new California boyfriend named Paco who was incredibly cool (he drove a '56 Cheby—that's how Nicole spelled it—and had "you wouldn't beleeve the neatest tatoos on his hands") and so she would not be coming to Oklahoma for a visit that summer. But now here she was, back again, with her hair even whiter, if that were possible, and her boobs even bigger, which was certainly possible because Lyla Mae could see the gargantuan evidence for herself, and her speech peppered with phrases like "groovy" and "bummer" and "no, man, listen, it was really far out."

If she hadn't hated Nikki so much, Lyla Mae might have felt sorry for her. After all, out in California things were happening. *Time* and *Life* and Scott McKenzie kept the whole world informed about how summertime was one big Happening out in California, and young people flocked there by the thousands from all over the country (although not, from what Lyla Mae could understand, to the town of Visalia, where Nikki and her mom lived), and here was poor Nikki, Grapes of Wrath in reverse, shuffled off to Oklahoma for the summer. It was too delicious.

"I don't suppose there's a snowball's chance in hell we'll be able to cop any grass down there in Bumfuck, is there?" Now Nikki was more or less eating her cigarette smoke. She'd released a great puff, not blowing out on it but just letting it come out of her mouth and stand in the air. She was opening and closing her mouth on it, like a fish on land, gasping for air. It looked pretty gross.

"No," Lyla Mae said. "Probably not." She would not let a trace of shock register on her face, no matter what outrageous thing Nikki might say. Nikki was unmerciful to her when she showed herself to be shocked.

It wasn't the notion of Nikki smoking pot that bothered her anyway, it was the way she used that word as a way to describe Cedar. Actually, Lyla knew about grass. Actually, Lyla had every intention of trying it sometime, and one of these days she would, too. But it wasn't going to be in Cedar, she knew that for a stone cold fact, and it wasn't going to be in the company of her cousin, either.

"No. I thought not. Man, it is going to be one bummer of a summer." Nikki punched her cigarette out in the overflowing ashtray and turned toward the window.

Lyla Mae felt again the heat of shame. She hated that Nikki could make her feel that way about Cedar—no matter how Lyla herself might privately think of it. No matter if she did groan inwardly and try to plead her way out of it, begging instead to stay over with her best friend Verna Wadley every time her parents announced they were "going down home next weekend." Lyla was embarrassed to be taking Nikki to a town where the boys all still wore their hair shaved up around their ears and slicked back with grease. Lyla had seen the pictures in the magazines. She knew what the boys in California looked like.

Nana and Grandpa were standing beside their blue Ford Fairlane when the bus stopped on the highway in Cedar. Nana's head scarf was tied loosely around her stiff bonnet of gray hair and Grandpa wore his straw dress hat pushed back from his brow and his suit jacket unbuttoned, though his skinny black tie remained closely knotted around his throat. When the bus door wheezed open, a great blast of scorched air surged upward against Lyla Mae's legs, swelled under her culottes, rushed against her face. She jumped down the steps, hurrying away from the clammy stink of air-conditioned smoke, the disturbing sense of blood-hot air pushing against cold, into the pure, parched sunshine.

"Welcome, welcome, welcome, welcome," Grandpa said, his preacher voice trailing out dry and feathery in the heat. He coughed lightly against the back of his hand. Nana hugged each of them in turn, and Lyla wondered what in the world she must think, both of them stinking to high heaven like old ashtrays— she could smell it herself, clinging to her skin—but Nana never said a thing.

As the Fairlane turned off the highway onto the main street of Cedar, Lyla Mae gazed at the storefronts lined up on either side of the street: flat cardboard cutouts, bleached, two-dimensional, wavering in the sunlight. She looked at the pickups angled nose-front against the high sidewalks like old bag-o'-bone horses tethered there. She looked at the square old post office and the bank, the pool hall and Tink's Hardware and Alford Mercantile, all of them sliding past the Fairlane, unreal, fake-looking, old and ignorant and ugly.

Lyla Mae hated Nikki again in one sudden rush.

Often in the evenings Lyla Mae wondered what sin she'd committed to justify such a sentence: an entire summer in Cedar with her cousin Nicole May. She doubted she had the strength to survive it. She expected to keel over any night now, her legs stiff in the air, dead from the agonizing effects of too much boredom compounded by one too many exclamations of "Man, what a bummer!" Lyla wrote Verna Wadley all about it. She and Nikki took walks, sat on the rock wall at the schoolhouse, did their nails. It was the closest thing to unbearable Lyla Mae had ever known.

One evening they were hanging out at the schoolyard, sitting on the wall in the long sultry twilight, picking at each other,

Nikki chain-smoking Winstons, Lyla Mae gnawing the polish off her nails, both of them restless, irritated, sweaty, sulky, and bored. It was Saturday night. They'd been in town for over a week.

Larry and D.H. DeWitt drove by, honking their ridiculous horn, waving their beer cans out the window.

"Who's that?" Nikki said. She pulled a cigarette from the pack in her lap to light with the butt end of the one she'd just finished.

"Oh, *them*." Lyla lifted the hair off her neck, twisted it up into a french roll, let it fall. She eyed Nikki's red pack of Winstons. "That's just D.H. and Larry. I wouldn't bother myself about *them*."

"Yeah? And why's that, Miss Know-Everything?"

"No-account," Lyla said. The DeWitts had been around forever, as long as Lyla Mae could remember. She'd seen them every summer of her life, hanging around the pool hall, cussing, spitting tobacco juice on the sidewalk when they couldn't have been over eight or nine years old. One time D.H. had come by the house on a no-account errand for his no-account daddy and caught Lyla Mae hunting Easter eggs with her younger brother. He'd nearly laughed himself sick. Lyla Mae couldn't stand either one of them.

"That redheaded one's kind of cute."

"I *doubt* it," Lyla said. "You don't know, man. He's a De-*Witt*." (That word—"man"—had crept into Lyla Mae's vocabulary somehow. It showed up in about three-quarters of her sentences. She couldn't seem to make it go away.)

"Oh," Nikki said. She breathed out a long sigh and uncrossed her legs.

Next it was Dubb Jenkins and Tommy Joe Bledsoe. They wheeled through the circle driveway, tires spitting gravel, radio blaring, both of them yelling out words Lyla Mae could not understand.

"Who's that?" Nikki whispered, leaning toward Lyla. Lyla could smell the dusky smoke on her breath.

"Nobody," Lyla said. "Dubb Jenkins and Tommy Joe Bledsoe.

I don't know 'em. Dubb's daddy's the Church of Christ preacher.
Tommy Joe's worthless. Dead meat anyhow. He dropped out of
school."

Sonny Lewman actually stopped long enough to toss out some
empty Coors cans. He was alone in his truck, and he didn't look
over at Lyla or Nikki. But when he peeled out he managed to lay
down an impressive amount of scratch.

Just about every boy in town who hadn't gone off to the war
or down to McAlester looking for work seemed to find his way
by the schoolhouse that evening. By the time dark came on, the
parking lot was jammed with pickups. Young men in blue jeans
lounged on dusty fenders, slouched against wheel wells,
crouched in the dirt. It was the most amazing thing Lyla Mae
had ever seen. Nikki kept leaning over to Lyla and whispering,
"Who's that? Who's that?" Lyla would give the rundown on the
boy's reputation and family history if she knew it, which fre-
quently she did.

"How do you know so much about this hick dump?" Nikki
said, and Lyla felt the old rush of defensiveness and shame.

"I don't know, I just know things. I keep my ears open, for
one thing. Shut up."

Lyla really didn't know how she knew so much about the people
of Cedar. It seemed like knowledge of the families was part of
the air of the town: you breathed it over pot roast on Sunday, on
the front porch watching fireflies, in the pews of the church. Lyla
thought you'd have to be deaf or dead to not know about the
people of Cedar, or else never have stepped foot in the town.
Nikki was showing off again, acting like her own ignorance of
Cedar proved she was sophisticated; the fact Lyla could tell histories, of course, just showed what a true hick she was. A surge
of defiance ran up Lyla Mae's backbone, jammed her lips shut,
lifted her chin. The next time Nikki leaned over with her smoke
breath and whispered, "Who's that?," Lyla Mae whispered back,
"Whyn't you go ask him." And when Butch Kirkendall opened a

beer can and handed it to Nikki, then punched holes in another one and held it toward Lyla, she hardly hesitated a second, hardly had time to catch the look in Nikki's eye, before she wrapped her fingers around the beer.

"Whadyathink?" Nikki whispered, nudging her in the side with her scrawny elbow. "That dark one over there, in the back of that black truck, he's kinda cute. If he'd let his hair grow out."

"Are you kidding?" Lyla whispered back. "He's a *Holbird,* for God's sake." Immediately she felt guilty for taking the Lord's name in vain.

"A what?"

"A Holbird."

Nikki looked blank.

Lyla Mae sighed. "A Choctaw." Nikki just looked at her. "An *Indian,* Nikki."

"So what?"

Lyla looked up at the stars. They shrank away from her like cellophane pinpoints, swooped low again overhead. "Never mind," she said, and took another swallow of beer.

"Well, what about that other one?"

"Which one?" Lyla tried to focus her eyes.

"That one there with him, the tall one."

Lyla sucked in her breath. "Oh, man," she said. "You don't want to mess with him. That's Ronnie Selby. He's got to be, I don't know, at least twenty years old. And he has a very bad reputation. A very. Very. Bad. Repu . . . ta . . . tion." Lyla's tongue had somehow grown a fur coat.

"Mmmm-*hmmm,*" Nikki said, and stood up. She handed her beer can to Butch Kirkendall hulking next to her on the wall. "Here, Budd," she said sweetly, "would you hold this a sec?"

Nikki made her way over to the black pickup.

.   .   .

When it finally occurred to Lyla to ask someone what time it was, it was already well past ten o'clock. "Oh, shit," Lyla said (and was amazed to hear the word come out of her own mouth). She finally located Nikki sitting, legs crossed, on the tailgate of the black truck. Ronnie Selby stood on one side, Hubert Holbird on the other. All three of them were laughing.

"Nick," Lyla said (and wondered where *that* came from, and how it could slide out of her mouth so friendly and easy), "we got to get home, man. We're gonna get *creamed*."

"Don't sweat it," Nikki said, laughing, tossing back her blond head to swallow her beer.

"Yeah, babe, don't sweat it," Ronnie Selby said.

Lyla Mae hated that word, "babe."

"Ni-*cole*," she said, not looking at Ronnie, "it's after ten o'clock. Grandpa's going to have a high-rolling fit."

Nikki stood up immediately, handed her beer can to Hubert, and started off across the parking lot. Lyla Mae hurried to catch up with her.

They were more than halfway to Nana and Grandpa's when the black pickup screeched up behind them.

"Hey," Ronnie Selby's voice said from the dark. "Hey, y'all girls. We're headed down to Woolerton afterwhile for the preview."

Lyla Mae kept right on walking, but Nikki slowed down.

"Saturday night preview. Down at Woolerton. Starts at midnight." The truck crawled slowly beside them. Ronnie's voice grew smoother, softer. "Hey, it's just a picture show. Hey. Y'all girls want to come?"

Lyla's footsteps dragged.

"We got to be in," she heard Nikki saying.

"Suit yourself." An empty beer can plinked on the roadway, rattled on the stones.

"We were supposed to be in at ten," Nikki said. She had stopped altogether. Lyla Mae looked back over her shoulder. She could

see the outline of Nikki's narrow hips, cocked to the side where
she stood with her weight on one leg, her elbow resting on Ronnie
Selby's door.

"Y'all always do everything you're supposed to do?"

Lyla couldn't hear Nikki's answer.

"What about your friend there?" Ronnie's voice grew louder
for Lyla Mae's benefit. "Hey. You. Little'un," he called out, the
sound of it rippling smooth through the night air, "Come on back
here."

Lyla Mae stopped, looked back at Nikki, and turned around.

When they came blinking their eyes into the yellow-lit living
room, Nana and Grandpa were watching the end of the ten o'clock
news. Lyla let Nikki do all the talking. Nikki said sorry they were
late, they lost track, they'd be more careful next time. She said,
yes, they'd had a good walk, it was a real nice evening out, and
no, no, they hadn't seen anybody to speak of, and well, yes, she
guessed it *was* hot, come to think of it, but not really so bad.

Nana looked up from her crochet then and sighed a little and
said, "Well, but you girls are young yet. Somehow a body just
don't mind the heat when you're young." Grandpa coughed once
and nodded.

Lyla and Nikki in turn both nodded agreement, yawned, said
goodnight, and went into the front bedroom, where they shared
the big four-poster bed that had once belonged to their great-
grandmother. They sat on the edge of the bed in the dark and
listened for Nana's gentle snore to start up in the near bedroom
and Grandpa's dry little cough to wind down in the back.

Then they crawled out the window.

Lyla Mae was never certain who came up with the idea that first
night, who first said the words. She couldn't recall how she'd
come to believe, in fact, that it was a bitchin' idea. Her memory
had the fused unreality of dream. Later, she and Nikki would

become slicker, more cautious. They'd stuff house robes and nightgowns under the bedclothes. They'd cram their mesh curler caps full of empty orange juice cans—that's what Nikki rolled her hair on to make it hang straight; she'd had to quit ironing it, she said, the ends were splitting practically up to her eyeballs— and arrange them on Nana's giant feather pillows. They'd take the old wind-up alarm clock with them in Nikki's leather-fringed handbag to make sure they got home no later than three.

In the mornings Lyla woke up sick to her stomach. Guilt like gray gauze held her face to the pillow. Sometimes her head hurt from the beer.

But by the end of the eternal hot afternoons, sitting under the gurgling water cooler with Nikki watching *General Hospital*, parading the dirt path across Nana's sideyard into town, swamped by the heat rising in waves from the blacktop, numbed by the monotonous chiding of locusts, bored to the point of death or of screaming, Lyla Mae was ready for the night.

After supper, as the sun began its slow downward slide to hide behind the humpbacked mountains west of town, Lyla and Nikki walked to the school. They'd perch on the rock wall in the twilight and watch the pickups drone to the end of Main Street, flip a U, come toward them to circle through the school driveway, drone away again down Main Street, making the drag. When the trucks began to stop finally, just after dark, and the Cedar boys, one by one, disgorged from the cabs, Nikki would say to them, "Hey, man, what's happenin'?"

"Pickin'," they'd answer, "just pickin'," kicking their boots in the gravel. Everybody was bored.

They'd sit on the tailgates and talk—or rather Nikki would talk, mostly, and everybody else would listen. She'd mention casually how it was never this friggin' humid out in CALIFORNIA, how there weren't this many mosquitoes to suck the blood out of you out in CALIFORNIA, no ticks or chiggers either for that matter, how it was never this friggin' boring out in CALIFORNIA. She never said "Visalia" or "back home" but always "out in CALIFORNIA," like the whole damn state belonged to her, according to Lyla Mae.

Nikki and Lyla made sure to be in the house by ten. They'd watch the news with Nana and Grandpa, wait jittery and silent in the dark bedroom till the snoring started, and then sneak out the window. Every night.

Usually they just went out to the strip pits with Ronnie Selby and Hubert Holbird, Dubb Jenkins and Sonny Lewman, and sometimes the DeWitts tagging along. The bunch of them would hang out, chunking rocks into the dark water (miles deep, Dubb Jenkins said: if you drowned in there your body wouldn't come up for months, they'd have to just go on and have the funeral without you), drinking beer, talking. In the cool darkness by the water, the stars hardly moving on the strip pit's black face, Nikki would often grow quiet. Then the boys would talk softly—about getting out of Cedar, about the war maybe, quitting school, getting drafted, sometimes about the weather or cigarette brands or nothing at all. Sometimes they'd get crazy, chasing each other up the shale hillsides, leg-wrestling, horsing around. All except Ronnie Selby, who was too cool to do that, and Hubert Holbird, who sat always a little off to himself, quiet, nursing a beer.

The boys never messed with Lyla Mae and Nikki. Lyla had a sneaking suspicion that Ronnie and Hubert had somehow staked them out. But the strange thing was, they never messed with them either. It was peculiar, in Lyla Mae's limited experience. Ronnie and Hubert certainly *seemed* normal—except that normal for any living breathing human boy she'd ever gone out with in her hometown of Bartlesville meant a mouth full of wet jabbing tongue and what Verna Wadley liked to call Roman hands and Russian fingers.

Still, Ronnie nor Hubert either one ever made a move. Lyla and Nikki discussed it in whispers out on the front porch after supper. Lyla told Nikki how Ronnie Selby got his bad reputation from having an illegitimate baby by some girl over near Poteau. She said the only thing *she* could figure was he didn't want to get a worse reputation by messing with the Baptist preacher's granddaughters, even if Grandpa had been retired from the pulpit for almost five years, and Nikki said she doubted *that* had anything to do with it. Nikki said maybe he was a secret fairy, and Lyla Mae said he had a *baby*, nitwit, so she certainly doubted *that*. Then Nikki sighed and rolled her eyes and said well she could hardly care less anyhow, she had a boyfriend out in California who was lots better-looking than Ronnie Selby.

On Saturday nights Ronnie Selby showed up late. Some of the other guys, too, wouldn't appear until nearly ten or even later, and Nikki and Lyla might end up spending the whole of Saturday evening talking to nobody but Hubert Holbird and the DeWitts. Lyla knew the boys of Cedar had girlfriends. She would see the local girls in town on Saturday afternoons with their hair in brush rollers. Nikki and Lyla would put their heads together when they passed on the sidewalk and whisper and laugh.

"I wouldn't be caught *dead* with my hair in brush rollers on Main Street, are you kidding?" Nikki said.

When they sat on the wall in the Saturday twilight, Lyla imagined Ronnie Selby driving out to the country to have supper at his girlfriend's house. She'd picture him and the faceless girl watching TV with the family after supper, see Ronnie take the girl, her hair fresh-washed and curly, out to his pickup—

Lyla's imaginings generally went dark and vague at that point. Ronnie Selby's reputation made whatever he did with his girlfriend in his pickup unsavory, mysterious, unthinkable.

One Friday night, the last Friday night in July, the whole crew of Cedar boys, Ronnie included, was down at the schoolyard at dusk. Lyla thought it was strange that the usual slow twilight stream of vehicles flowing along Main Street had gone still. Instead, pickups and cars crowded the school lot, and the boys of Cedar stood around drinking beer, talking softly, kicking their boot heels on their fenders. But when Nikki said, "Hey, y'all" (she'd copied that "y'all" from Ronnie Selby, because nobody in CALIFORNIA said "y'all," Lyla Mae was just pretty sure of that fact), "what's happening?," they all drawled back, "Pickin'." Same as always. And then laughed.

Ronnie and Hubert were waiting for them in the black pickup at eleven that night, just like always, when they crawled out the window and walked to the corner. The truck coasted without headlights until they reached Main Street, and then peeled onto the asphalt with a terrible roar. When they pulled into the school-yard, a dozen other pickups were there.

"I swear to God," Nikki whispered, leaning into Lyla Mae's ear, "if I never see another goddamn pickup as long as I live, it'll be too goddamn soon."

"Yeah," Lyla said. "I know what you mean."

But Lyla felt good. She was halfway through her first beer and the night was starting to cool down and it was still long many hours yet before the secret dawn when she'd wake up feeling wrapped in gray gauze and burning sick in her stomach and afraid. She had on a new pair of silky blue bikini underwear, bequeathed to her by Nikki in one of her strange fits of generosity, and her hair, for once, was flipping under instead of up. Lyla felt sure that the thing she'd always known about herself was true: one of these days she was going to *be* somebody.

"Y'all ready for this?" D.H. DeWitt leaned in the window of the truck, grinning, showing his brown gums.

"I'm ready for anything," Nikki said.

"Ready for what?" Lyla said.

"Ready to head out to the country." D.H. turned to spit snuff juice onto the gravel.

"I'll tell you what," Nikki sighed, "I'm ready for *some* kind of happening around here. This dump is getting on my nerves."

Lyla Mae felt her teeth grind down and the back of her neck stiffen. There it was. That was the very kind of thing she just hated about Nikki.

She would get to the place sometimes where she thought she could actually tolerate another month of living with Nikki. When they were alone together Nikki would often make little jokes, or she might ask Lyla Mae's advice, like which eyeshadow looked better with her outfit or something. But then they'd get out in public and Nikki would go into one of her eye-rolling oh-I-am-just-so-bored-I-could-die routines, or else she'd start using some word Lyla Mae didn't even know what it meant, like "psychedelic" or "paraphernalia," and then sigh like Lyla Mae was the most ignorant human being on the face of the earth and say, Oh, you know, it just means, like, far out.

"Yeah," Lyla said. "Right. Ready for anything. Me too," and she scooted across the seat to follow Hubert Holbird out the door.

When everybody loaded up into two pickups, most of the guys riding in back with cases of beer iced down in washtubs, Lyla Mae didn't think much about it. When they drove out along the highway and then turned off onto a dirt road headed toward LeFlore County, it was still nothing new. It was just like heading out to the strip pits, only with a bigger party.

Ronnie's pickup rumbled along the dirt road. Wolfman Jack was howling on the radio across all those miles of night sky between WLS in Chicago and Laminer County, Oklahoma. Lyla Mae thought about how teenagers in Chicago and Kansas City and New Orleans and who knew where-all else were every one listening to Tommy James and the Shondells at this very minute. Any one of them could look up and see that exact same three-quarter moon that she could see jouncing along the horizon just over Nikki's right shoulder. She might even meet one of them someday, and neither one of them would ever know that one July Friday night long ago they had both been listening to Tommy

James and The Shondells and looking at the exact same moon at exactly the same minute. It was very strange to think about.

The music faded out as Wolfman came howling back in, and the night wind sailed in the window, mild and damp, a balmy salt wind drifting up from the Gulf. Lyla thought with a sudden shiver that no matter what, no matter how awful it might get in the daytime, an Oklahoma summer night was the most exquisite thing on earth. She felt itchy with excitement, as if any kind of miracle thing might happen at any moment and every particle of skin on her body knew it. At the same time, she felt terribly relaxed. She reached up and took a Winston out of Nikki's pack on the dash.

The dirt road wound along the valley floor between the dark shapes of mountains. Just before they hit the county line, the pickup turned off onto a dusty two-lane track. They bounced along, the headlights from the other truck jiggling behind them, sawing the night air, lighting up the field. They were on old man Bethel's place. Lyla Mae recognized it immediately. She'd come here with her grandpa a dozen times in her life, and once or twice with her daddy, always for the same purpose: to buy watermelons. Old man Duke Bethel had the finest melons anywhere around.

"What's up?" Lyla said, laughing a little, putting one hand up to the dash. She didn't like the way one world was crashing into the other. She didn't want to be drinking beer with a bunch of Cedar boys in old man Bethel's watermelon patch on a Friday night in July.

"Oh, just pickin'," Ronnie Selby said, and laughed.

They loaded up Ronnie's truck bed with watermelons. Lyla didn't help pick them, but Nikki did, traipsing along the rows in the dark, giggling. Lyla Mae could see the orange-red tip of her cigarette bouncing up and down. "What a hoot!" she heard Nikki laughing. "Man, they'll never believe this when I tell them out in California!"

Lyla stood in the dusty track, drinking beer. This is *stealing,* she kept saying to herself, I can't help it, man, this is *stealing.* But she didn't say it out loud. She kept imagining scrawny old man Bethel in his sweat-stained felt hat, bending over like he'd always do to lift away the scrambling vines and show off his melons.

Oh man, Lyla said to herself.

They took the melons back to town and broke them open on Main Street. Lyla Mae sat in the truck while the Cedar boys and Nikki ate old man Bethel's stolen watermelons. The melons made a terrible sound when they smashed onto the pavement. The boys scooped out the red heartmeat with their fingers and laughed and spat seeds at each other and slurped melon flesh into their mouths. The busted rinds they left scattered on the street, jagged-edged, spilling juice. The boys of Cedar thought it was a whopping good time. They thought they'd created a Happening.

Larry DeWitt came up to the open door of Ronnie's truck, where Lyla sat listening to the radio. "Whatsamatter, church girl? Ain't you hungry?" He grinned at her, his pointy chin shining.

"No, I'm not hungry. Not for some kind of stolen watermelons." The beer was making Lyla Mae feel bold.

"These ain't stolen melons," Larry laughed, "These melons is just temporarily borrowed." He turned around and wandered back into the street.

Lyla Mae turned the radio louder. After a bit Ronnie Selby's hand reached in and switched off the key and pulled the keys out of the ignition.

"You trying to give me a dead battery?" he said. "Can't get out of here with a dead battery in case the law shows up, can I?" His voice went soft and insinuating. "Can't drive out to the strip pits later."

Lyla scooted across the seat to the other side and shoved the door open and climbed out of the truck.

Nikki came swaying up, her blond hair shining white in the street light. "Oh man, I just thought of something. I just now thought of this, man. Listen." She leaned her bony forearm on Lyla Mae's shoulder. Her breath smelled sweetly sour, like melon and beer. "Listen to this, man. Can you imagine if we were born in April? They'd have named us April, like April Nicole or April Mae—or no, listen to this. What if we were born in *June*? Lyla June! Don't you just love it? I mean, is that hicky or what?" Nikki leaned back against the pickup, laughing. "Lyla June! What a hoot."

"Yeah, well, what if we were born in September," Lyla said, and walked away.

She was sitting on the high sidewalk in front of Alford Mercantile dangling her legs over the edge when Hubert Holbird came up to her with his hands cupped around a piece of watermelon.

"Want some?" he said in his low, shy voice.

Lyla Mae ignored him, but he went on and sat down next to her anyway, holding the dripping melon away from his knees. He didn't say anything more.

After a long time sitting in silence with Hubert, watching the others party in the middle of Main Street, laughing, splatting melons, swilling beer, Lyla Mae finally turned to Hubert and asked him, "How come they did that?" When Hubert still didn't say anything, she said, "I mean, how come old man Bethel's melons? Why not Floyd Waters' or somebody's? At least Floyd Waters is a real prick." That really wasn't what she'd meant to say at all.

Hubert looked at her. Then he laughed once, a soft sound, almost silent, through his nose. He kept looking at her, like she knew the answer if she'd open her brains once and think about it. Finally he shrugged his shoulders. "Bethel's got the best melons," he said, and took a bite out of the piece he held in his hand. He said it like he was saying when it rains it gets wet.

Ronnie Selby came up to them then with a whole melon in his arms, cradling it like a baby. He touched Hubert's foot with the side of his boot, and Hubert stood up, nodded at Lyla, and drifted over toward the pickups.

Ronnie sat down and planted the watermelon on the pavement between his boots. "What's the matter with you?" he said.

Lyla didn't answer.

"You scared your old granddaddy's gonna find out?"

Lyla still didn't say anything.

"Let me tell you something, babe," Ronnie said, leaning back to pull a jackknife loose from his front pocket. "Your granddaddy has stole his own share of melon in his own time. Don't let anybody kid you."

"That's not it," Lyla said softly, but now the thought of Nana and Grandpa finding out made her stomach turn over, jellylike and cold. "Listen," she said, starting to stand up, "we better get in. It's probably, God, after three o'clock or something."

Ronnie took hold of her hand and pulled her back down to the sidewalk. "Sit," he said. He flipped the knife open and carved a deep slice out of the melon. "You better have a taste of this." He put the dripping melon into her hand, wrapped her fingers around it with his, and lifted it toward her mouth.

The melon was sweet, warm from where it had been sitting in the July sun all day, liquid. Lyla Mae swallowed. Ronnie pulled her hand away and tossed the melon out into the street. His hands were wet and a little sticky when he touched them to her cheeks, and his mouth was warm and sweet and liquid when he leaned down to kiss her. But he only stayed there a moment. Then he stood up, stretched his arms over his head, said, "Come on, little'un. We better get back over there 'fore they drink up all the beer."

He reached down to help her up, and when Lyla raised her

eyes, her hand rising to meet Ronnie Selby's, she saw her cousin standing behind him.

Nikki had a thin gash of melon in one hand, a burning cigarette and a Coors can in the other. Her legs were spraddled, arms rigid, jutting away from her body like the frame of an A. The streetlights and beer put slack in her face, turned it ropy and hollow like the face of an old woman, but it was the expression there that startled Lyla so that her raised hand fell back limp, unwilling, to her lap. Nikki looked like a child. Her eyes were fragile round circles. Her mouth puckered. Her brows curved, lifted, came together in the middle of her forehead to form a question. In a small voice she said, "Hey, y'all."

"Hey," Lyla whispered, and as she watched, Nikki's face changed again, transformed, looked satisfied, as if the single event she'd been expecting had come to pass and now there was nothing more to wish for. She lifted the corners of her lips at Lyla and turned around to walk back toward the trucks.

When the law came, Lyla Mae was sitting on the tailgate next to Ronnie pretending to smoke one of his Camels. Nikki was in the cab of the other truck making out with Sonny Lewman. Dubb Jenkins and Hubert Holbird were drunkenly pitching quarters on the sidewalk. Larry DeWitt was passed out in front of the pool hall; ditto for D.H., sprawled across the seat in Ronnie's cab. The rest of the Cedar boys had gone home a long time ago.

"Oh man," Lyla said when she saw the white cruiser pull up.

"Shit," Ronnie said, and then, "Be cool. Be cool."

Hubert hollered, "Selby!" by way of warning, leaped over Larry DeWitt's passed-out body, and took off running. Dubb Jenkins followed, stumbling quickly behind.

Sonny's and Nikki's heads bobbed up over the seat back when the sheriff's radio squawked as he opened the car door.

"Be cool," Ronnie said softly to Lyla, "Just be cool."

The sheriff got out of the cruiser and came walking toward them.

"Evening, officer," Ronnie said, standing up, shaking his jeans legs down over his boots. "Something I can do for you?"

Lyla Mae looked at the street littered with beer cans and smashed watermelons. She looked behind her at the twenty or so stolen melons crammed up next to the cab and the dozens of empty beer cans floating in the washtub in the truck bed. She looked at Larry DeWitt snoring face-up in front of the pool hall and Sonny's and Nikki's bleary faces peering out the truck window. And she thought, Oh man. It is just no use.

Lyla Mae and Nikki spent what was left of the night sitting up in hard straightback chairs in the lobby of the Laminer County Courthouse in Woolerton. The sheriff tried to make them call Nana and Grandpa themselves, but they both refused, Nikki sitting stiff and stone-faced in her chair, Lyla crying and hiccuping and shaking her head. Finally the sheriff dialed Cedar just before daylight.

Lyla Mae couldn't decide which moment was worse: seeing Grandpa walk in with his black tie neatly knotted and his straw dress hat turning around and around in his hands, or later, when old man Bethel came through the glass doors in his felt hat and overalls, shuffling his great feet, ducking his head, not looking at Grandpa.

They stood like own kin in front of the sheriff's desk, both of them looking frail and thin and old and a little bewildered. Lyla Mae watched Grandpa's face. How did he get so tired-looking and old? she thought. Suddenly she knew she hadn't looked at him all summer. She hadn't seen how it had happened that her blustery preacher granddaddy had dried up somehow into this thin yellow-faced man with the dry little cough. Lyla's chest tightened, the gray sickness swept over her. She looked at Nikki, but Nikki was gazing out the window, fidgeting with her fingernails.

Old man Bethel refused to press charges, even against Ronnie and Sonny and the DeWitts locked up in the rock jailhouse out back.

The sheriff rolled back in his chair and crossed his fingers over his belly. "Well, now, Reverend Muncy," he said, "considering that these are your granddaughters here"—he nodded in the direction of Lyla and Nikki—"and seeing as how Mr. Bethel here don't want to press charges"—he nodded at old man Bethel— "so my hands aren't tied, so to speak. And considering that nobody likes news like this to travel around much . . . well, I don't know . . ."

The sheriff rubbed the sagging skin beneath his eyes with his thumb and forefinger, then pressed down on his closed eyelids.

"I was thinking. I might not have to charge these boys back here with contributing to the delinquency of these minors"— another nod at Lyla and Nikki—"we might just slap 'em with a little loitering and littering charge." He paused. "If that'd suit your mind. So to speak."

Grandpa nodded his head, thanked the sheriff, and led the girls out into the burning sunlight to the blue Fairlane for the long quiet ride back to Cedar.

The judgment against them was not a blustering tirade, as Lyla had secretly hoped for, but a pained, bewildering silence. Nikki herself wasn't speaking to anybody, and Nana spoke little. Grandpa was steadily silent, sitting in his chair staring at the television, coughing, leaning over now and then to spit in a can. About the night before, nothing was said. Nana told the girls at supper that Lyla's parents would be down from Bartlesville to pick them up after church the next morning. She said Nikki would take a plane back to California Sunday night. Those were the only words spoken that even partway alluded to the girls' shame, but a few times Saturday evening Nana came up to Lyla and put her hand on her forehead and brushed the hair back and kind of smiled at her. Once she said, "I know y'all are good girls."

And dozens of times throughout the night on Saturday, Lyla heard Nana get up and come to the door of Lyla and Nikki's bedroom to check on them.

It was then, too, late in the night, that Nikki started to talk. She hadn't uttered a word in all the miserable hours since the sheriff pulled up in his cruiser, but in the pale moonlit darkness when Lyla Mae wanted only to cover her face and mind with Nana's feather pillow and forget, Nikki talked.

"Goddamn stupid hick Okies," she whispered, "goddamn stupid stupid stupid goddamn stupid goddamn."

Lyla stared at the blurred ceiling, taut on her back, hating Nikki.

"Goddamn stupid goddamn stupid stupid stupid," Nikki whispered, and Lyla hissed through her teeth, "Shut up!"

Nikki was quiet for a time, and then she said, "Man. Nobody is going to believe me I got kicked out of Oklahoma for stealing watermelons. Nobody. God. What a bummer."

"So lie," Lyla said, and turned over on her side to face the window. "Shut up, Nikki. I'm going to sleep now."

But it was Lyla Mae who was lying. There was no way under heaven she could get to sleep, and she knew it. She'd slept the whole day. She'd walked into the house behind Grandpa and Nikki in the morning, walked quickly past Nana without looking at her, directly into the front bedroom, and crawled into the bed and turned over and fallen straight to sleep, only to waken in the blue wash of twilight confused, remorseful, sickened near to death in her soul before she wafted close enough to consciousness to remember what she should be so sorry and sickened about.

The moments just before waking were always the worst. Lyla lay still now, staring out Nana's lace curtains at the sideyard lit bright in the moonlight, thinking about that. It was like her conscience knew wrong before awareness took over. Like her soul's mind told her the truth of matters while it was still pure and close to God. Lyla thought back to the first morning, the first dawn after the first time she and Nikki sneaked out of Nana and Grandpa's house. She thought how the gray gauze had been wrapped around her already when she jerked into wakefulness, how she'd recognized it immediately, known it was guilt. How she'd never once waked up feeling sick and scared before that morning, and how she'd been waking up that way every morning since.

It was just one more reason to hate Nikki.

"Lyla?" Nikki said.

Lyla ignored her.

"Lyla? Know what? When I get home I'm going up to Frisco and cop some grass. Me and my friend. We've been planning it all last semester. Want some? I could mail you some. Lyla?"

Lyla lay rigid.

"Lyla? Listen, it's no big deal. We snuck out of the house, stole a few friggin' watermelons. Big deal."

Lyla whipped around in the bed. "Shut up, Nikki! God, can't you ever for once just shut up?"

The bed started shaking then, a soft undulation, and Lyla thought Nikki was laughing at her, silent, holding the sound in. Lyla turned over, sick with hatred and rage, and faced the window again. But then she heard the faint whisper of Nana's slippers on the living room linoleum, and she rolled over once more and grabbed Nikki's thin arm, squeezing it under the sheet, digging her nails in. Nikki held still, and Lyla kept her eyes closed, but she sensed Nana in the doorway. Nana turned away finally, and Lyla heard her slippers scuffing away across the living room. She released her nails from Nikki's arm. Nikki's breath exploded into the room in a long ragged shudder.

"God, Lyla, rip my arm off why don't you? Jesus."

"Quit taking the Lord's name in vain," Lyla said into her pillow.

"Oh," Nikki sucked in her breath, "aren't we Little Miss Goody Two Shoes all of a sudden."

Lyla was silent.

"I guess I didn't see you sitting in the street making out with Ronnie Selby, did I? I guess you're just the heighth of innocence and perfection like everybody in this friggin' family thinks. Too good to eat some old hick's watermelons."

Lyla stared at the pale filmy curtains with the memory of Ronnie's mouth and the sweet warmth of the melon rising in her, and the way she'd swallowed, partaken of it for no better or clearer reason than that Ronnie's hand had placed it against her lips. She willed the memory away, but it clung to her, soft, insistent.

"Too good for anything. Give me a break." Nikki's voice went on, shaking, the words chopped by quick shudders so that Lyla knew that Nikki had not been laughing at her but crying without sound in the dark. "Chickenshit's all I'd call it. Man. I can't believe this dump. I can't believe this family. I can't wait to get out of here, you can't get me on that plane fast enough. Stupid. Goddamn stupid stupid stupid, I can't believe it, when I get back out to Cal—When I—"

The room was suddenly quiet. Crickets chirred their nightsong in the sideyard. Lyla heard the slow pulsing of blood in her ear pressed to the pillow. She felt Nikki beside her, shaking the bed, panting short squeezed-out breaths, and then Nikki's voice came again, almost a whisper, saying what Lyla had never imagined.

Like how she didn't really feel much like going back out to California because she hated it out there because namely her mother had a new boyfriend who was an out-and-out creep who kept trying to feel her bra strap through the back of her blouse, and because it was just going to be a bummer in Visalia because there wasn't a goddamn thing to do until school started because Visalia was nothing but one boring stupid town like one big fat useless raisin and she hated her whole stupid life and wished she could start over or else quit because in the first place her mother couldn't care less whether she lived or died and everybody acted like she was so dumb or else just pure wicked and if she didn't grow some flesh on her stupid bony legs she didn't know what she was going to do because she had the ugliest chicken legs on the face of the planet and she was sick to death how everybody thought Lyla Mae was so perfect, how everybody thought Lyla Mae was so goddamn smart and pretty and perfect and kept throwing her up to her like she was some kind of goddess, wanting to know why can't you be like Ly-y-yla, why don't you do good in school like Ly-y-yla, stay out of trouble like Ly-y-y-yla, it was enough to make somebody vomit.

She was quiet for a time. Lyla lay still, trying to comprehend what she'd just heard. Finally Nikki said, "Those guys, all of 'em, they think you're some kind of friggin' mystery woman or something." She quit talking again. Lyla heard Ronnie Selby's black pickup rumbling along Main Street, turning at the schoolyard, peeling out onto the asphalt, laying down scratch. Nikki said, her voice very thin in the dark, "What I want to know is, how do you all the time just sit there and not say anything and everybody thinks you know so much or something. I mean, how do you just *sit* there and not talk?"

Lyla couldn't answer her. It had never occurred to her that sitting around not knowing what to say could ever be a good thing. Nothing had ever occurred to her, she thought now. Or at least nothing like Nikki was saying. She'd never imagined anybody thinking such things about her. She'd always felt herself to be practically invisible, a watcher sitting quiet on the wall, looking, waiting to see how to act. Certainly she'd never thought that Nikki, Blond-Know-It-All-Big-in-the-Boobs Nicole May, could hurt on the inside or hate how her legs looked or feel stupid the way Lyla half the time sat around feeling stupid. She couldn't imagine that Nikki had actually compared herself to Lyla. She'd never fathomed the strange awful truth that she and Nikki were alike in some way.

Nikki's voice came again, light and airy now, only a little half-hitch of sob at the back of it. "Anyhow," she said, "I knew all along Ronnie Selby had the hots for you. Huh. Pure Okie. Needs a little Brylcreem I guess, that one. Needs some more glass packs for his hick pickup truck."

As if in answer, Ronnie's pickup squealed around the corner onto the unpaved road in front of the house. The familiar thundering sound of the engine barreled through the screen. Lyla lay stiff under the starched sheet, sweating, listening to Ronnie's truck rumble to the corner, turn around, drive, slowly, loudly, past again.

"What in the world does he think he's doing?" she whispered to Nikki. "He's going to get us creamed for sure now." Lyla's heart beat fast, only partly with fear that Nana and Grandpa would hear. "He's nuts. What's he doing? Nikki?"

No answer came from Nikki's pillow.

Lyla whispered again, "Nikki? What's he trying to prove? He's going to get us annihilated. Nick?"

But Nikki had gone silent again. She stayed that way through each of Nana's soft-scuffing night checks, through Lyla Mae's sighs and tosses and turns and low whispers, through the rumbling of Ronnie Selby's pickup back and forth in front of the house, back and forth, all through the night.

1970

H ubert Holbird heard about it from the front steps of his grandmother's house at Blue Hill. His cousin Tinyboy Morrison walked the six miles from Cedar to tell him the news. Hubert heard the dogs yip under the house and tumble out barking in the yard, and he looked out the window to see Tinyboy in his big hat and small boots walking up the dirt road. Walking slow in the cold bright noon sunlight. Hubert stepped out the door then to wait on the cinderblock steps in his shirtsleeves for what Tinyboy had come to tell him.

Tinyboy stood in the yard with his thumbs hooked in his belt buckle, talking of other things. Said it was plenty damn cold for the end of March, wasn't it, he'd never seen a thing like it, he hadn't seen a tree one that had started to bud. Hubert said he reckoned it would warm up sometime. Tinyboy said, well. He kicked a smooth depression in the dirt and rocks of the yard with the toe of one boot, a boot scarred and handsome, hardly larger than a child's. He said, you working? Hubert said, some, said he'd cut wood for Pinch Kirkendall last week. Tinyboy nodded. Hubert watched the hole growing softer and deeper. Tinyboy said he'd busted his damn wrist that last go-round in Montana, he'd had to lay off rodeoing for a while. Hubert didn't answer. The boot scraped back and forth, back and forth, a sound like dirt clods thunking steady against dirt. Tinyboy said, how's Ida, and Hubert said, fine. He said, how's your sister, and Hubert said he hadn't heard from her in a while. Tinyboy said, well. He took his hat off. His face seemed to jump forward in the sunlight. His black hair was clamped in a ridged circle. He stepped back and looked up at the sky, squinting.

"Well," he said after a while, "I reckon it'll have to warm up sometime."

He looked down at the hat in his hands. It was dusty and dimpled, his saddleback-bronc-riding hat. Hubert watched him smooth the redtail hawk feather in the hatband with his fingers. Then Tinyboy began turning the hat by the brim, around and around in a circle.

"Well," he said. "Just thought I'd let you know." He put the hat on. His face fell back in shadow. "Heard in town this morning Ronnie Selby bought it in Nam."

For a moment Hubert Holbird thought he might let himself think Ronnie Selby had sent a souvenir by way of Tinyboy, a trinket, a small Vietnamese statue or ashtray he'd bought somewhere in Quang Tri.

Hubert's grandmother came to the door then. There was a soft sucking sound when she pulled the wooden door inward, a light twang as she pushed out on the screen. She stood between the two doors with her head dipping toward them.

"H'lo, Aunt Ida," Tinyboy said.

"Tinyboy," Hubert's grandmother said. It was quiet a moment. Hubert felt his grandmother's eyes watching the both of them. After a while she looked only at Tinyboy. "When'd you get in?" she said.

"Couple of days ago."

"From Montana?"

"Durant. I's just down at Durant. Little horse-breaking job."

"I thought you was in Montana."

"Well," Tinyboy said, "I was."

A shrill garbled crow came from the back of the henhouse.

"Come in," Ida said.

"That's all right, I just come by to tell Hubert something. Piece of news I heard in town."

Ida was silent. Tinyboy stood looking off toward the henhouse where the old loco rooster had flapped up into the elm tree and was crouched there. Crowing at noontime.

Hubert stepped down off the cinderblock into the yard. "Ronnie

Selby got killed," he said, and walked away around the corner of
the house toward the woods.

He stayed in the woods for four days. He told himself he was
hunting, though he had no gun, no buck knife, not even a piece
of string to make a trap with. In the beginning he simply walked,
in the mountains south and east of Cedar, his mind blank and
his feet propelling him forward without pattern or purpose, just
a slow steady walking, through pastures and bramble fields, up
hillsides and down ravines and along the sliding muddy bottoms
of creeks. But on the morning of the third day a need came on
him to do something. He did not know what it was he could do
but the need was inside him, and he tried things. He walked to
the south branch of the Little Fourche and checked his trotline,
found a couple of perch and a big carp still living and a dead
catfish, took them off the line and threw them back in the water.
He walked to the old places on Blue Hill behind his grandmother's
house where he'd built shrines as a boy, small secret places where
he'd piled rocks and animal bones and pieces of foil and feathers,
but there was nothing left—only in one place some dirty chewing
gum wrappers, in another the thin gnawed white skull of a coon.
   He hiked to the top of Big Ridge, where he could see the
Kiamichis blue and misty rolling off to the south, or stand where
he was, cold, the sky burning, and turn and see the Sans Bois
humpbacked and shimmering to the north. He walked along the
top of the ridge where Horace Bledsoe had sprayed the trees with
poison and cleared it after the trees twisted brown and died and
now kept his cattle. The steers walked beside him, bawling.
   Hubert looked in the clear cold spring light to the mountains
south and north, the long valley east and west, and said to himself,
I should stay here on this ridge. I should *do* something. But he
didn't know what it was he should do, and so could not, and he
scrambled down the far side of Big Ridge, cutting his arms on
the brambles, tripping on the jutting slabs of sandstone, pushing

through the scrub oak. He dug sharp-edged blue cedar berries from beneath the needles with his fingers, the way they were, round in the center and pointed in hard stars at the end like a foolscap, and he bit them, hard and dry and bitter in his mouth, and thought, *I am hunting.*

Hubert walked out of Laminer County, walked south through the mountains nearly to Talihina, and when he recognized the pink neon lights of the High Life Dancehall and Bar and the thin strip of blacktop in front of it shimmering pink below him, he stood for a while, looking. Then he turned around and went home.

When he came in the house at near dawn, his grandmother was sitting at the table by the coal-oil lantern reading her Bible.

Ida stirred only a little when Hubert came in. She didn't raise her eyes or lift her head from where it was bowed over the pages, but there was a soft stirring in her, a shifting, a recognition. She went on reading, moving her finger along the cramped lines, her lips trembling silently. She began to whisper softly the words of the Scripture, but Hubert said, "Ida!," his voice cracking in the quiet, and she stopped and stood up and went to the cookstove.

"You want frybread or biscuits?" she said, and reached into the woodbox for kindling.

"Nothing," Hubert said. "I'm not hungry." He sat in the cane-bottom chair by the window and bent to pull off his boots.

"I guess you are," his grandmother said quietly. "I guess you just don't know it."

She sat at the table again and went on reading, or seemed to, though her lips were still and her finger did not move on the page. After a long while with no sound in the room but the thin hiss of the lantern, she stirred again, a slow sift of her black skirts, and said, "Funeral's Friday."

Hubert shrugged his shoulders once and shook his head. He turned to look out the window where the day was seeping gray and the elm by the henhouse just taking form.

"Son," Ida said, and Hubert turned again to look at his grandmother. Her face was peaceful in the lamplight. Her hair was
loose on her shoulders, the few threads of white blended dark in
the shadows. The lines in her cheeks were smoothed to nothing;
her eyes were brown and still. "There's reasons for rituals," she
said. "The Lord knows. He gave us these forms for healing. He
heals every pain."

Hubert turned back to the window, and the elm was now stabbing its stark and bare fingers against the lightening sky. The
loco rooster began to crow. It's not that, he said to himself, though
he would not say it aloud to his grandmother. It's not that.

His grandmother's voice came into the room behind him, first
a whispering, then a low murmur. " 'I will ransom them from
the power of the grave,' " she murmured. " 'I will redeem them
from death. O death, I will be thy plague. O grave,' " she whispered, " 'I will be thy destruction.' "

They held Ronnie Selby's funeral in the Cedar High School auditorium because there was not a church large enough, not even
the First Baptist, to hold all the people in the town. Hubert Holbird
and his grandmother walked the six miles to Cedar in the sudden
warmth of that Friday morning, her skirts swirling dust on the
back road, his boots tapping chinks in the silence when they
reached the highway and walked west along the blacktop shoulder into town.

Hubert stood in the school parking lot and waited. He watched
as his grandmother's black head scarf and skirts disappeared
into the darkness through the large double doors. He listened
to the organ wheeze and groan into the silence, the sound of
the hymns, the marching music, the preacher's voice rumbling.
He listened to a girl's voice begin moaning, rise to a shriek, and
subside.

He listened, but really he heard nothing, and it was only later,
remembering, that he could tell what he'd heard. He stood in the

parking lot and leaned against the hot door of a pickup, leaned in the sunlight and waited.

The coffin seemed large on the shoulders of the soldiers when they walked out into the light with it draped in a flag. The coffin seemed large, but weightless and empty, and other flags went before it, carried on staffs, flattened in the heat and the unmoving air. The VFW flag, the Masonic, the American Legion. The flag of Cedar High School, a limp flap of purple. The United States flag, red and white stripes collapsed together. The flag of Oklahoma, its round Choctaw shield, its peace pipe, crimped and twisted inside the blue folds.

Hubert dropped back into the shade of a pine tree and watched as the procession moved toward the black cars. Behind the flags and the coffin walked the pallbearers—the few Cedar boys left in town not drafted or still in high school or sent to prison at McAlester or dead: Butch Kirkendall, Harriman Ryder, Soak Waters, Leroy Laney, D.H. DeWitt looking badly hung over, stumbling in the rear—pallbearers in name only, with no job to perform because the military bore the coffin. Behind the Cedar boys walked the family, Ronnie's father, thin and crumpled, his mother facing forward, back straight, lips tight, eyes blank, in her small veiled black hat. Ronnie's young brother Wade walked slowly, formally, behind his mother. He stopped suddenly, stark still, and the townspeople bunched up behind him. Wade stood with his neck stiff, his head jabbing forward, staring hard in the shadows at Hubert Holbird. A look that said, where the hell were you. A look of pure hatred and blame. Hubert drifted back further, and Wade stepped fast to catch up with his mother.

The townspeople milled out in the parking lot, the procession broken now, like a kicked-over anthill. Allie Alford and Cotton Sanger, Granny Ryder, Eunice Mabry, Stump Wilson, Silas Tarplin, all the old ones and the young ones, and the middle ones who carried the business of Cedar on their backs. Hubert's grandmother was small in the midst of them. Tinyboy walked beside her in his big dusty saddleback-bronc-riding hat. Several girls bunched together in the auditorium doorway, trying to outweep each other and moan. Two girls fainted, one after the other, and there were little stirs of commotion in two places as the girls were revived. A few men pulled out cigarettes or plugs of tobacco and stepped off to the side. And then at once the people of Cedar swept together and moved forward to the black cars where the soldiers were lowering the coffin from their shoulders. The soldiers' faces were turning red with the strain.

Hubert's mind began then to break free of waiting, but it wouldn't stay in the present or pay attention or help him. It slid backwards, remembering, and Hubert thought of the bonepickers, old Maytubby's stories of the bonepickers. Hubert laughed almost at the sight of the soldiers straining with the coffin. They slid it into the hearse like there was weight there, the weight of ten bodies, but Hubert knew better. Ronnie Selby had been dead several weeks. He'd been blown apart anyhow.

Hubert Holbird followed the funeral procession. He moved through the long afternoon shadows like a day haunt, passing swiftly from sideyard to sideyard, from pickup to hillock to pine, drifting farther and farther back but following relentlessly the mile-long line of cars and trucks with lit headlights trailing the three black limousines behind the black hearse driving slowly west and north from Cedar along the gravel road to the cemetery at Bull Creek. But it was seven miles to Bull Creek. By the time Hubert cut through the high brittle weeds in Faulk's pasture and arrived at the sandstone fence surrounding the cemetery, it was near dusk and Ronnie Selby was under a brown hump of earth. The military was gone. The family was gone. A man in a black suit was rolling up a green tarp. Hubert stood outside the fence and watched the funeral parlor people pull multicolored wreaths from the back of the hearse and lay them on the fresh dirt. The colors were garish against the raw earth. A few townspeople walked about in the twilight, wandering between the headstones, bending their necks to murmur to one another, pausing to read names.

Hubert came from behind the rock fence and knelt beneath the bare spreading arms of an oak tree some little distance away from the grave. He watched the heap of flowers rise higher, the brown hump being hidden beneath bright streaks of gladiolus and mums, satin lavender ribbons, silver letters, yellow sunbursts, carnation flags of red, white, and blue. The softened voices of the men from Seedly's, the faint mosquito hum of the meandering townspeople, murmured at the edge of Hubert's being. Memory stirred in him, indistinct memories from his boyhood of sunlight and wood pews and his hands fidgeting, his legs cramped and aching, the sound of hymns, and the Choctaw preacher's voice, his grandmother's voice, rising in him, whispering words of faith and redemption and escape from death into life everlasting.

As Hubert watched, the colors on the grave turned iridescent in the twilight. On the hillside behind the cemetery the hollow *oowah oooo oooo oooo* of a mourning dove echoed from the trees. Another memory brushed over him, faint, like a wisp of cobweb walked through in darkness: the memory of Maytubby sitting in his smokehouse telling stories. Hubert saw him, the old man's hair short and steel-colored, sticking up stiff from the top of his head, his voice moving slow, his fingers swift on the lattices, weaving new seats for cane-bottom chairs. The cane slats rippled through Maytubby's fingers like snakeskins, forming shapes, and the smell in the smokehouse was of roots and hog slabs and the earthen floor where Hubert, a boy then, a small child then, had sat.

In the fading light, with the mauve sky darkening to purple and the townspeople's voices disappearing in the violet on the far side of the cemetery, the old words began to come to Hubert. He heard Maytubby talking, part English, part Choctaw, telling how in the old time in the old place when the dead had been long dead on the burial scaffold, the flesh rotted and settled and the time for mourning fulfilled, the family of the dead would send for the bonepicker. How the bonepicker was not a spirit but a Choctaw man of flesh and honor, with fingernails grown to lengths of four inches, a Choctaw man of honor in the tribe. How it was the bonepicker's job to climb to the top of the scaffold and pick the decayed flesh from the bones of the dead one, as was honorable and sacred. How in the old time the bones would be buried by the people in the place with the bones of the ancestors, to be kept and honored in the burial place by the living Choctaw for always.

A sharp click sounded in the evening quiet. The men from Seedly's walked from the closed rear door of the hearse to the two front doors and got in the front seat. The last of the towns-people made their separate ways back to their vehicles and climbed in and coughed their engines awake. They lit their lights and drove off south behind the hearse on the gravel road toward their lives. None of them once looked at Hubert.

He sat beneath the oak tree and watched the first star steal through the blue on the northern horizon. He watched the colors on the earth fade to humped smudges and bleed into black as night came and there was no moon. The whippoorwills started, relentless, unceasing. Then silence as the night chilled and deepened. The milky sweep of stars overhead crystallized into separate frozen pinpoints. Hubert felt his eyes pierce the dark mound of polystyrene and plastic and living petals. He could see in the darkness through the tan rocks and dirt, past the silver skin of the coffin into the sealed black place where Ronnie Selby's body should be. But the place that held Selby's body was a torn mat of hair and chalk and splinters. There was no Selby here. There was nothing to bury. Hubert Holbird, surprised even as he spoke them, not knowing where they came from, said the words of Christian burial.

" 'Dust thou art,' " he said aloud in the darkness, " 'and unto dust shalt thou return.' "

Hubert told himself there could be no death here because there was no body to disintegrate and turn back to the earth.

He raised his eyes.

In the dark space in front of him Hubert saw a bonepicker climb to the top of a scaffold to take the rotted flesh from the bones of a dead one. He saw the bonepicker scrape the bones hard and dry and sacred with his fingers, saw him paint the skull red and fix the bones in a woven basket for the long wait, the burial.

The picture, when Hubert saw it, was ancient inside him—as if it had been his from his boyhood, and on backwards, back beyond that.

1976

*S*elena Sikes Willaman had held all her life an abiding horror of irrevocable acts. This fear of taking any step in the world that could not be turned back upon had kept her a virgin until well past her twentieth birthday and unmarried until she'd almost reached thirty. It had kept her from ever finally making up her mind to have children (because what if you had one and it turned out to be horrid?) and prevented her from her one great dream of seeing Europe (because—oh, this was the stuff her nightmares were made of—what if you got over to Italy and a war started or something and you could never, ever get back). Her fear kept her from moving away from the tiny town of Cedar and getting the education she wanted and doing the things in the world she knew she could do.

She, of course, was the only one who knew she was crippled, because the people of Cedar, as she so often had to tell herself, had no ambitions of the mind or the heart. They thought Selena was perfectly successful because her team of eighth-graders won second in the statewide debate contest three years in a row. They thought that because she sang in the church choir and taught Sunday School and had managed to stay slim when every other woman in the town had gone to fat, she'd reached the pinnacle of achievement. But Selena knew the secrets of her own heart and knew how little, really, she'd ever done in her life because of fear that it could never be undone once it had got started. So when she ran off to New Orleans with the new young Freewill Baptist preacher, abandoning in the process his young wife and her old husband and six children between them, no one was more surprised than Selena herself.

Three of the six children, to tell the truth, were John Willaman's grown kids by his first wife, two of whom already had children themselves, but Selena had to include them when she was reading off her list of sins to herself. She did read that list, over and over, as she and the preacher drove south through East Texas in perfect silence. Oddly enough, adultery was way down at the bottom and seemed to her to be one of her lesser transgressions. The sex between them had been so inevitable, so involuntary and necessary, like breathing, that she couldn't somehow find the proper shame to attach to it. But lying to everyone and sneaking around, abandoning John Willaman—who had always been good to her—and his three grown children, forcing the preacher to abandon his little dopehead of a wife and their three toddlers, all these things she believed she could feel ashamed of. She added the bad example she was setting for her eighth-graders to the list, and the fact she was shaming John in his own town. Sometimes she included for good measure—though she knew it had never been listed as a sin in the Bible—the shock she'd be delivering to all the ladies of her Sunday School class when they found out, then tacked onto that sin the dubious trespass of causing those same ladies to commit the sins of gossip and wrath and, quite possibly, envy.

Selena mulled over her list in the silence. She tried to acknowledge the depth of her iniquity. She felt she ought to own all the proper amounts of shame attached to it and her due portion of guilt, like a dull sickness in her chest. But though she did manage at times to conjure up shame, to feel it fiery in her cheeks and along her breastbone so that she knew she was not without conscience, Selena could not seem to drag up repentance and, try as she might, she could not find remorse.

Outside the window, great stern trees stood draped and bearded in moss on either side of the road, their trunks black and separate, knee-deep in water, and their boughs tangled together in the gray blur overhead. A thin fog clouded the far end of the highway so that they seemed to be always driving into nothingness and yet never arriving there.

But when she looked over at Brother Stephen's pale face, fine-boned, slightly frowning, she remembered the reason she was riding in a car hundreds of miles away from Cedar in a strange part of the country she'd never heard of before. He would turn toward her from time to time and smile or reach across the seat to touch her hand. Then Selena would take the heat of him in through the skin of her fingers, and the small flickers of shame in her chest would turn to wanting. It seemed, in those moments, that her perception of the world came only through the dry, slight touch of his fingertips. His hands were long, pale as glass, and soft, as a preacher's hands should be soft, not like any man's hands that had ever touched her before. The hands, she thought. It was always those hands. And she would sit for a time breathing the world in through the skin of her fingers.

Then Brother Stephen would pull his hand away to put it back on the steering wheel, and Selena would be left with the open ache of wanting, helpless and unsatisfied, so that finally she'd turn toward the window again and begin her silent litany of sins. She gave herself up to the little hidden surprise, the concealed pleasure, that she had actually done such a thing, and sometimes she mused (though not very seriously, and these were the only times she came close to her usual habits of thought) on the possibility of there ever having been a moment when she could have turned away and not done what she had done.

She thought of the first time his eyes paused on her face (stopped, and stood still for just the space of a breath, looked long and deep and secret into her eyes) as he paced in the pulpit delivering his sermon on a Sunday morning. She wondered lightly if that might have been the moment when she could have turned aside. But she could not take her eyes away from him. It was never possible for her not to look back. She knew that. She thought of the moment, standing near him in the church office with the amber autumn light falling across the floor from the high window and the Sunday morning bulletins flap-flap-flapping on the mimeograph machine, when she first saw the softness of the skin on his neck, saw the small intricacies of his tiny, perfectly formed ears, and felt her lips, the tips of her fingers, aching to touch him. She knew that even then, long before the cold evening in the car on the way home from prayer meeting when she reached up with her fingers to touch his cheek, it was already too late.

When was it? she thought, joking with herself, because she knew there had never been a moment of turning back. The first minute I laid eyes on him, she almost whispered. She thought of him standing in front of the altar with his little blond washed-out wife and their blond fidgety toddlers to be introduced to the church, and Brother Stephen with his impossibly black hair and his black eyes burning in that white face, so long-legged and gangly and awkwardly graceful in his perfect blue suit. Selena smiled at the fog-shrouded highway. She knew she could only have been saved if she'd never once seen him, if he'd never been called to Cedar, if she'd never gone to church. She shifted on the plastic seat, smiling, and turned to look at him.

His face was outlined against the whirling gray of the passing countryside, high-bridged nose standing out strong and elegant in relief, slick strands of black hair dipping over his forehead. The white of his skin looked like wax in the wintry light. It had always amazed her, his skin, the way it could look so cool and dry and fine, and then turn to fire under her lips. No, it wasn't his hands, she thought, it was that skin. Nothing that white should have so much fire inside it. She reached up with the backs of her fingers to brush against his cheekbones. He smiled, his eyes on the road. Look at me, she thought, turn and look at me.

But the preacher kept his eyes on the highway, and Selena, retreating from the ache of unanswered wanting, turned once again inward. They drove for hours in silence that way, with Selena counting up her sins and the young preacher thinking

whatever mute thoughts he was thinking and the misty East
Texas winter rushing past them in judgment.

In the thickening gray that signaled the approach of evening,
they stopped for dinner at the Pizza Hut outside Jasper, Texas.
The young woman who waited on them there had recently had
her left hand cut off—the stump was still swathed in bandages
—and somehow the sight of that irrevocably removed hand (or,
more accurately, the lack of the sight of it) brought all of Selena's
old terrors thrashing to the fore.

She smiled a great deal, at the waitress, at Brother Stephen,
and tried very hard not to look at the stump, but inside her chest,
her heart seemed to have given up beating.

"Y'all want large or medium on that?" the waitress said, and
smiled down at Selena, whose own smile was frozen like a waste-
land across her face. Selena turned her frozen smile on Brother
Stephen and nodded for him to answer. It mattered not at all to
her, she wasn't going to be able to swallow a bite in the first
place.

The waitress marked the slot on her pad for a large Supreme.
She was really very good. She balanced a tray upon the stump
and kept it from wobbling by the judicious pressure of her breasts.
Her order pad was on the tray and she used a little stub of a
pencil to mark down the order. When she'd finished, she poked
the pencil behind her ear, clapped the tray against her chest with
the stump, and smiled down at them. "Right back with your
coffee," she said, and walked off.

Brother Stephen stood up, excused himself awkwardly, and
walked back toward the restrooms. Selena sat in the booth and
stared at the waitress as she read the order off to the boy ladling
sauce onto pizzas in the back. She's so young, Selena kept saying
to herself, she's so young for that to have happened. But Selena
knew it wasn't just the girl's age that wrenched her stomach and

squeezed shut her heart; it was the fact it had happened recently. The bandages, so clean and white and gauzy, propped under the tray, sickened Selena in a way that a naked, healed, flesh-colored stump never could have. To think, Selena said to herself, that no more than a few weeks ago that girl had a hand. She had one, like anybody has one, and then, suddenly, she didn't. How was that possible? How could you have one, and then not have one? How could you wake up in the hospital without it and know in one horrifying heartbeat that you'd never, ever have one again?

A slight moan slipped through Selena's closed lips.

The waitress came toward her with two cups of coffee and two glasses of water balanced on the tray. When she reached the table, she held the tray steady with her breasts while she lifted the cups and glasses. Selena smiled at her again, and turned to look out the window at the parking lot.

Brother Stephen came back and slid into the booth opposite her. After a while their pizza came and he ate it while Selena stirred her black coffee and stared at the dull cement and faded white lines in the parking lot. Once, she looked up and found his dark depthless eyes burning into her, and Selena felt her mind go blank and cold in some kind of startled confusion, but then he flashed his eyes and his old boyish grin at her, taking her with him in the old helpless way, and said, "You feeling all right, Selena?" Selena nodded and said she was fine, just not very hungry, and pulled a slice of pizza onto her plate in order to please him.

They never mentioned the girl's missing hand, never acknowledged the fact of it with their eyes, not even when she came to remove their half-eaten pizza and the tray slipped off her stump and clattered onto the table scattering crusts and clumps of sausage all over. She filled up their coffee cups, shy and embarrassed, and smiled awkwardly when she slid the check onto the table. "Thanks a lot," she said. "Y'all come back." She moved up to the front, where Selena watched her talking softly with the boy behind the counter. How could you ever talk to anyone again? How could you ever do anything again except sit and stare at the walls in stark holy terror? A cold wash of revulsion and fear slid over Selena and she smiled over at Brother Stephen and said, "You about ready?"

The preacher's young face seemed to be getting younger and more bewildered by the minute. He nodded and reached across the table for her hand, but Selena slid it from beneath his and reached for her purse.

As they drove east toward New Orleans, Selena felt herself wrapped around in darkness. The wipers smeared road film in a great oily streak over the windshield, blurred the oncoming head-lights, and distorted the blackness, so that only the inside of the car seemed to be moving through space.

"I should've thought to change yours and mine both," Brother Stephen said.

Selena looked over. The glow from the green panel lights al-ternated with the slow sweep of headlights on his face.

"I don't know how come me not to think of that." His voice barely rose above the sound of the engine, the wet rush of tires.

Selena was silent. There seemed to be something she'd for-gotten, but she couldn't focus her mind on what it was. She only felt the steady thrum of the motor driving them onward and the gaping sense of wet, empty night all around her.

"Them blades," the preacher said. "I should've thought to do that," and his voice was hurt, insistent.

"Yes," Selena said.

His fingers touched the back of her neck, brushed her skin softly, a slow gentle circle sliding up under her hair.

"Yes," she said again, and felt the warmth of him drawing her, pulling at her from out of the darkness. When she looked up, she believed she could see the city of New Orleans ahead of them, though she knew they were still hundreds of miles away.

She thought she could see the soft, pulsing glow of it on the horizon, drawing her to itself. The pull of the city and the warm, secret pull of the preacher sitting next to her in the car seemed to be two halves of the same power, sweet and dark and compelling, drawing her down. She thought she could drown in it, melt into it, lose her soul and her self into it forever. She did not struggle.

When he turned off the highway onto a soft, marshy side road and switched off the motor, Selena only sat waiting. And when he reached over and pulled her toward him, she went to him with no bones in her body, nothing firm to resist him, but only the soft yielding of her being, folding into him. She touched him, trembling, cherishing his skin, the touch of it on her lips, the taste of it on her tongue. She ran her tongue over his nipples, tiny and pink and hard, like a child's, and felt him shudder beneath her. This, she said, just this, just this, and her mind would not think.

But in the damp gray light of dawn, when they pulled into the motel parking lot and she saw the whorish fluorescent lights flashing pink and green along the motel roof, and later, when they stood in the shabby yellow room and she saw the knife holes, hundreds of harsh, thin slits stabbed helter-skelter into the peeling yellow pasteboard over the bed, the surprise and the horror came on Selena, and she knew she had committed an irrevocable act.

The knife holes were, she thought, the element that broke her, broke into her and made her pull back and recognize her madness. It had all been madness, of course, extreme and insane and inescapable, like a spell laid upon her, and now there was never, not ever, any turning back. The narrow slits kept drawing her eyes, seemed to glare, slant-eyed, at her from over the bed. They looked as if someone had played mumblety-peg against the wall, and there was such a corruption about the thoughtless way they were stabbed there, such a total disregard for property or sense or order, that Selena thought they exactly stood for the tawdriness of the room and the corruption of the gray sleeping city all around her. She hated them. She could not look at them without thinking of that knife flying across the room, stabbing into the wall, vibrating there. Of the same hand (whose hand had it been? what bored or menacing or insane man had stabbed that wall so many times?) pulling the knife from the wall, over and over again, only to let it fly and stick and vibrate once more. The cold metal glint of the knife in her mind's eye was equal to the cold metal slicing machine that had taken the waitress's hand (and it did not matter that she didn't know in reality what had happened to the girl's hand: it surely had been robbed of her by something metallic and glistening and sharp).

Selena could not sit down in the room, could not bring herself to touch the sheets or the ancient bathroom fixtures. She felt Brother Stephen's eyes following her as she paced back and forth, into the bathroom, out of the bathroom, to the ugly door with its peeling list of rules and its deadbolt, around the sagging bed to the far back wall and the high window blocked up with an air conditioner, back to the bathroom and out again. If she stopped for a moment, she felt the germs in the room—other people's germs, how many hundreds of other people's germs—would swarm her, crawl onto her skin and seep into her pores.

Selena's fears had caught up to her. She did not know what she was doing in a cheap motel room hundreds of miles from Cedar with a stranger, some strange, unknown black-eyed stranger.

Brother Stephen reached for her as she raced past him, caught her and pulled her to him, held her tight against his chest, and she felt his heart racing against her breastbone, pounding against her, an insane, quick, tormented rhythm. He took hold of her shoulders then and pushed her away from him, held her there. Selena looked up at him out of a blankness. The flashing lights outside the window gave the only color to the gray light in the room. They played over the preacher's face, lit up his pale skin in alternating pink and green washes, buried his eyes deep in shadow.

"Selena—" he said, and then let go of her shoulders and stepped back away from her. Selena saw him for a moment, almost a boy, confused and unsure, waiting for something from her. And then the veil fell again, and Selena thought only of the fact that she had never once called him by name.

Late in the night her husband came to her in a dream and stood around in the motel parking lot, waiting for her. Selena rose from the harsh damp sheets and went to the window. The parking lot was slick and black with rain, and John Willaman was not there. But still she felt him, and she went into the bathroom and turned on the water in the shower stall and stood in it, smelling the rust and the mildew, wanting the water, desiring it, while it gushed from the ugly shower head, pouring down, pounding down, hot and furious on her neck.

The heat of the water could not burn the image of her husband from behind her eyes. She saw his clumsy work boots shuffling on the asphalt, his shaggy big head tipped forward, bewildered, asking. She pressed her fingers against her breastbone, whispered a furious, silent no into the pounding wetness. She turned her face north and west, and saw the long black empty miles between her and Cedar. Her house, a low-slung brick ranch house, sprawled low on the earth outside of town. The highway unraveled backward, blue-black and empty, and she saw herself and the preacher in the gray, sinking place at the end of the land mass. The end of the earth, sinking into the sea.

"I did this," she said out loud in the shower stall. She saw every moment that could have been different, every look, every touch, that could have been left undone. She knew then how the girl at the Pizza Hut lived over in her mind, every morning, every

evening, those minutes before the accident, the whole day before
the accident, her whole life leading up to that irretrievable second,
examined every action and said to herself, If only, if only . . .

Selena stood in the water and watched herself sitting in her
pew on a bright Sunday morning, saw herself staring back at
Brother Stephen as he paced in the pulpit. She watched her cold
fingers in the dark car reaching up for his cheek. She saw her
husband hunched against the rain outside the motel room, shuffling his work boots on the slick parking lot. She would not say,
If only. "Madness," she said. But the word was not good enough.
Of course it was madness, crazed, hungry, insatiable madness,
but she could have turned aside from it if only she'd wanted. "I
never wanted," she said, and took the full grief and loathing into
herself with the words.

The water in the shower turned lukewarm. And then bone-
chilling, rushing, ice-water cold. Still, she stood there. Her limbs
went numb and dead with the coldness. She thought of Salvation,
and Redemption. She knew they were just words and had never
been real, and she hated that she had ever been taught them.
Because no step in the world could be turned back upon. No step
and no non-step ever allowed for turning back. John Willaman
sank away into the glistening asphalt, and Selena reached up
with her deadened fingers to turn off the water.

She stepped out of the bathroom, naked and wet and shaking,
her mouth shuddering, shoulders trembling, thighs and breasts
and arms trembling. The preacher stood in the middle of the
room. His narrow chest looked ghostly, sunken, in the streaming
light from the bathroom. He balanced himself awkwardly, his
long legs shy and dancing, as if he were ashamed of his naked-
ness. But when Selena looked at him she saw him wanting her,
straining toward her.

She went to him, hating him, hungering after him, and let him
wrap his long burning arms around her and pull her down into
the warmth and the sweet darkness.

1979

We started out bad together to begin with, but I didn't have sense enough to see it. I didn't have sense enough to see anything except that ring around my finger and I guess that's the way with any young flip-tailed girl who's dying to get married. I was—or thought I was, anyhow. I thought if my daddy wouldn't let me marry Clay Holloway I'd just as soon go on and die right then and be done with it. I was sixteen years old. Later I used to think Daddy would've done me a favor to put me in a toe sack and drowned me that day, saved both of us a lot of years of useless misery, but of course he didn't know anything either. Girls got married or else they got in trouble back then. That was all.

But things started off bad and went from bad to worse right down the line, and it wasn't just him drinking either. That's what most folks think, I know that, but that was just a drop in the bucket, just one little corner of the whole nature of the way things were between me and him, and if I was going to kill him for being a drunk I would've done it twenty-five years ago and not waited till he was near sixty.

It's hard to explain.

Seemed like he just wanted me to do everything for him, that was the main thing. Well, in the beginning, you know, you're willing to do everything. You *like* to do everything, you figure that's your job. It's all I ever saw my mama do and I never thought a thing about it.

But with Clay it was more than that. You'd have to know the man to know what I mean. Well, even knowing him wouldn't be enough I don't guess because he knew practically everybody in this county and still folks think I killed him because he drank or because he slept with that pop-eyed Janice Waters every Friday night off and on for fifteen years.

Truth is, I don't know why I killed him. But I'm trying to get to it.

Wasn't how hard he worked me, though I think I heard somebody say that. He did work me hard, rode me like a mule if you want to know the truth, started out that way from the beginning and never eased up a drop, but that's nothing new. Lots of women I know have worked like turks all their lives and they don't go around killing their husbands. It was something different.

Clay . . . he just wouldn't let up. I don't know how to tell it. You'd just have to know him. He wore me to a nub every day, and I don't mean working in the house or around the place, I mean something different. Ways I couldn't even begin to name. Like how he was about cooking.

He had to have three kinds of meat, scratch biscuits and gravy, grits, eggs, fried potatoes, cornbread and buttermilk and sorghum molasses every morning of the world. Well, we was raised like that, all country folks was, you had to eat like that to get the work done. But with Clay, even after the kids was grown and gone and the land had all been let out to Horace Bledsoe to graze his cattle and Clay himself was already big as the side of a barn, I still had to get up every morning at five-thirty to fix his breakfast. Well, that's not so bad. When you've been doing it all your life you can stand at the stove and stir grits in your sleep and not even hardly know you're doing it. But trouble was, I never could do it to suit him. Never. In all those thirty-four years of marriage there was something wrong every blessed morning of the world: the eggs was too done, the cornbread was too soggy, the damned sorghum molasses that I bought in a jar at Alford's store was too slow or too runny and even that was my fault.

In the beginning I figured he was right. I'd been helping my mama cook and clean and raise seven children littler than me since I was big enough to reach the stove with a stepstool, but I figured Clay knew more about everything than I did.

He was nine and a half years older than me. We got married at the justice of the peace in Woolerton and come on back here and settled in at the house and I hardly ever stepped foot out of it except to go to the barn or the truck patch for the next several years, and I didn't have an inkling it ought to be any other way. I thought Clay knew as much as God or my daddy. Don't laugh. There's women all over this country started out their marriages the same kind of ignorant as me.

That first morning—and I was still so scared, and hurting like the devil, which was one thing I sure didn't expect when I was so hot to get married. I'd been watching animals all my life and I never did see a female animal looked like she liked it much, but I didn't figure it could be too bad or so many women wouldn't be thinking that the end-all and be-all of existence was to get married to some man. My mama hardly got past explaining menistration, which only come about after she found my dirty drawers where I'd buried them out back by the smokehouse and the dogs had dug them up, so I didn't have much understanding as to what to expect.

But that first morning he got me up out of the bed at five-thirty to fix his breakfast, and I did it the best way I knew how, my chest all swelled up with pride and this notion about being grown up, a woman now finally, once and for all. And I kind of limped around the kitchen there, still sore between my legs, you know, and scared, but happy. And he come in from the barn and set down at the table—and started in on me. Right from the start. This is what I mean. If I'd had the sense God gave a horny toad I'd have turned and run every step of the eleven miles back to my daddy's house.

But what did I know? I didn't know nothing.

Lois, he said, from here on out I want sausage and bacon and fried ham all three when we've got 'em, understand?

Sure, honey, I said.

And I don't like my eggs scrambled. I want 'em fried in the sausage grease, understand? Not the bacon grease, the sausage grease, you hear me?

I didn't know what to think. He'd never talked to me like that, not once in all the six months we courted.

All right, honey, I said.

And make sure the yella is cooked soft. But not runny. I don't want to see any runny yella yolks on my plate, I can't stand that.

Yes, honey, I said.

He ate quiet for a while. Well, quiet's not hardly the word because there's not a human on the face of this earth ever made more noise eating than Clay Holloway, but what I mean is, he wasn't talking. Then all at once he threw his fork down and shoved the plate halfway across the table.

There's lumps in this gravy, he said.

Where? I asked him, and come over to the table to look.

He jumped up then, stomped his foot, I thought a scorpion'd got him. Don't sass me! he hollered. I'm not having no sassy damn wife. Did I tell you there's lumps? If I say there's lumps, there's lumps, and I don't want to hear any back talk out of you and I don't want to see any more lumps in my gravy.

He dumped the gravy bowl upside down on the floor and walked out of the house.

I should've run right then. I should've gone out the door behind him and never looked back. Instead of waiting around thirty-four years hoping he'd die.

He never did hit me much. Once when I didn't close the gate good and his Black Angus bull got out and in-pregnated half of Stump Wilson's herd for free and he couldn't get Wilson to pay him a cent because Stump said he never intended to mate those Herefords with a Black Angus and if Clay didn't shut up about it he'd make him pay to abort ever last one of them, and one other time just after Clay Junior was born, I forget now why. But he laid into me hard enough with his tongue down through the years to make up plenty for the fact he never beat me.

I was ignorant. I was stupid. I was fat. I was lazy. Mostly it was a matter of me being stupid. That was his biggest gripe, and most the time I believed him. Truth is, I *was* stupid. Otherwise how do you explain me staying with him all those years?

I left him one time.

That was my worst mistake. Everything changed after that, and I regretted it every day of my life from that day forward.

No. What I really regretted was going back.

How come me to go back was two reasons. First of all the preacher said I'd ought to. He said the wife was made a little lower than the husband to be helpmeet to him and I'd ought to return home and stop acting contrary. He said he'd pray for me. My family never went to church much when I was little, but along about the time I was pregnant with my third baby I started going into Cedar to the Church of Christ because it seemed to me like there had to be more to life than cooking and cleaning and having babies and taking whatever's dished out to you. Turned out there *is* a lot more, but you have to wait till you're dead to get it. But the preacher's words carried some weight with me, so I listened to him and let him pray over me there kneeling on my sister Frieda's front porch. I'd gone to stay with my sister. Preacher prayed hard enough for sweat to pop out on his forehead. I appreciated his time and attention, driving all the way out there to Frieda's, but I don't think he could have talked me into going back if it hadn't been for Clay himself.

Clay acted different than I'd ever seen him act in my life. He come in the back door there at Frieda's just weeping like a baby. It was ten o'clock in the morning and he was already drunk as a hoot owl. He got down on his hands and knees and begged me. He crawled all the way across Frieda's kitchen floor. Told me everything was going to be different from here on out, told me I

wasn't stupid but his good sweet smart wife. Told me I was a
good cook, if you can believe that. He just cried and carried on.
Said he'd give up Janice Waters, give up drinking, never, ever
lay into me again if only I'd just come home. Said my babies was
crying for me, which was a flat lie of course, because the only
one left at home was Sharon and she just liked a year being out
of high school. The worst part of it was he kept asking me over
and over again, why? Said he couldn't understand it. Why, Lois?
For God's sake, honey, tell me why.

All I could say to him was, well, if you don't know I can't
tell you.

But he just looked and acted so pitiful. Kept grabbing onto my
skirt. Backed me clean into the stove. Said he didn't know how
he could live without me. He reached up and tried to stroke my
hand. I jerked it back and he grabbed hold of my skirt again,
buried his face in it, rubbed it all up and down over his eyes till
the thing was wringing wet. Frieda's twins tuned up bawling,
Frieda started bawling, it was a mess.

And I went back, Lord help me.

After that, everything changed. And I mark the road to me
killing him from that date.

In the first place, that's when I started drinking. I'd never had
a drink of liquor in my life before that morning, but on the way
back to the house sitting next to him in the pickup I said, Clay,
hand over that bottle. Said, if you can stay drunk and ornery all
the time, reckon I can too. Well, he was too glad to get me back
to argue, and he handed it over. See, that's how it went. I started
out in that marriage a churchgoer and ended up a drunk, and
neither one helped.

Well, my daddy drank, you know, and so did my brothers.
There's always been just two kinds of folks around Cedar where
liquor's concerned—them that drink and them that don't. Them
that drink drink hard, and them that don't are teetotalers, and
that's always been the decent majority. But my daddy and broth-

ers was what you call binge drinkers, so I never saw it. I just knew daddy'd go off and stay gone for a month and come home puling and puking, and mama'd put him to bed and nurse him and I'd start school in last year's dress because he'd drunk up all the money. My mama never drank and I never knew a woman who did. So there wasn't any way for me to know in advance that I'd be as big a drunk as my husband if I ever got started.

I used to sneak around with it. Nobody ever saw me in a honky-tonk, nobody ever saw me buying liquor, which is why folks around here was so shocked when it come out in the papers I was drunk when I killed him. You can hide it a long time. Well, we lived so far out in the country, for one thing. Never had much company on account of Clay'd cussed out pretty near every one of the neighbors at one time or another, and the kids was all long gone, and mama and daddy'd been dead for years, so all that's partly how. And I still got up on Sunday mornings, washed my face and went to church, bought groceries in town every Saturday, continued on in the world same as Clay did, and I don't guess a soul knew, except Frieda says she suspected it all along but Frieda always acts like she's got the last word on everything so you can't tell.

The other thing that changed after I went back was Clay himself. I might could have stood anything but that.

I guess I scared him when I took off. I guess he saw himself getting older and fatter down through the years and his gout getting worse. He knew good and well Janice Waters wasn't going to take care of him. Maybe he just felt what it feels like to be alone. Who knows why he started acting like he did.

But he started calling me names. It was sweetheart this and honeybun that. Sugar, shug, sweetie, darlin', babydoll. It made you want to puke. And he never let me out of his sight. That was the worst part. He acted like we was joined at the hip. If I went out to throw peelings to the chickens, he stepped out on the back porch to watch me. If I went into town to buy groceries, he just suddenly remembered he needed to pick up something at Tink's Hardware, he might just as well go along. He even started going to church. Well of course everybody around thought he'd had a conversion, but the truth was he was afraid I'd go into town on a Sunday morning and never come back.

Now what would possess a man to act like that? Here he'd done nothing but heap abuse on my head from day one of our marriage, now all of a sudden he acts like he can't go to the toilet without I'm holding his hand. And don't think his mouthing at me stopped. It didn't. I still couldn't cook a meal to suit him nor iron a handkerchief. He'd go from hollering at me to sweet-talking me in the same breath. He'd say, Lois, get over here and help me tie up this bootlace. The man couldn't do a thing in this world for himself. I'd get down on the floor in front of him, he'd start complaining about the looks of the knot I was making the same minute he was trying to stroke me on the head. Made me just want to scream. I'd go in the pantry and take a little nip. Clay knew what I was doing. He bought my bottles for me. I think it just suited both of us better if I drank in the pantry.

I know folks are going to be shocked when they hear how we carried on. By suppertime I'd be meandering all over the kitchen. I quit even pretending to cook. Clay'd eat leftovers for supper and I'd go in and turn on the TV.

He'd come in with his beer and I'd head for the pantry. He'd follow me and stand outside the door hollering. Then he'd start honeying me, sugarbabying me.

I'd come out and go in the living room and he'd follow me. He followed me all over that house.

I kept a bottle in the bathroom, that's the one other place Clay wouldn't follow me. I hid it under the little crocheted toilet-paper cover Sharon gave me for Christmas one year. It didn't cover it good, but it covered it good enough.

He'd stand outside the door saying, honey, come on out now,

I need you to fix up my denture fizz for me, then he'd switch over to yelling. I'd sit on the pot and drink.

Afterwhile he'd go back to the icebox for a beer and I'd come out and head for the porch. He'd finally find me on the porch. Never failed he had to come squeeze his fat self right in next to me on the swing. Always had some little something he needed me to do for him. I'd go back and get in the pantry.

We just went on like that.

By bedtime we'd both be skunk drunk. Clay generally passed out on the divan. He'd wake up and pee and come on to bed about midnight. Some nights I fell asleep in my La-Z-Boy chair, but most the time I went on to bed.

And then come around five-thirty in the morning he'd be leaning over mouthing at me to get up out of that bed and fix him some breakfast.

I killed him over breakfast. I don't mean over the issue of breakfast, I mean right literally there over the eggs and grits and three kinds of meat. He keeled over head first at the table. His face wound up in the gravy. I thought that was pretty good justice at the time, but of course I was drunk.

I've been trying to recollect what I was thinking when I shot him. Seems like it might be important. Seems like if I could just remember that, I might could come to some kind of reckoning about how come me to kill him.

I remember feeling a terrible red-looking fury, but I believe that was all through the night before when I didn't go to bed but just stayed up drinking. I don't know why I didn't go on to sleep that night, I think I was just too mad. What's funny is that it wasn't anything special Clay did to make me mad. That day hadn't been any different from any of the rest of them. It was just all in my head.

But I stewed and fumed all through the night, talked to him in my mind all night, told him everything in the world I didn't

like about him. I'd flipped the vibrator switch on my La-Z-Boy—
the kids had all went in together last Christmas to get that vibrating chair for me—and I switched it on and set there with my
bottle. And I talked to him. Didn't say a word out loud, but I
talked to him.

Said, Clay Holloway, you're a worthless fat no-account lazy
stupid stinking helpless slobbering useless excuse for a husband.

Said, if you don't leave me some peace and quiet I don't know
what I'm going to do.

Said, you can't just come glom onto a person like an old gob
of spit and expect them to tolerate it.

Said, you just shut up with those words of yours, if I hear that
word sugarbaby come out of your mouth one more minute there's
no telling what I'm liable to do.

Said, you just learn how to cook your own breakfast, I'm sick
of it. I'm eating corn flakes from here on out and that's all.

I told him other things, I don't even remember now what-all
I said, while he laid there snoring on the divan.

I looked at him, looked at his fat belly blubbering and shaking.
White stubble poking out all over his chin. Seemed like I could
smell the stink of liquor coming out of his mouth. Seemed like
I could smell the stink in my own mouth, that was the worst
part. I smelt the stink in the both of us. Two of us stinking up
that living room every night till the end of it.

That's what made me maddest of all, that's when I shut up
and just set in my vibrating La-Z-Boy in a red haze of fury, looking
at Clay Holloway. Just looking at him and drinking. And then at
five-thirty I went in and fixed his breakfast.

By the time I got his shotgun out of the closet I don't remember
feeling mad anymore. Clay was sitting at the table. He hollered
back over his shoulder, said, shug, looka here, honey, I believe
you're losing what little mind you've got, you never put the cream
on the table. He'd shut up the noise of his eating just long enough
to say that.

I come into the kitchen, come up about five foot behind him, and raised the muzzle of that gun.

You know, for the life of me I can't recollect what I was thinking. I can see it plain as day though. I can see the way the back of his head opened up and everything spattered all over the floors and the walls and the icebox. I can see him falling forward and his face going splat in that gravy bowl.

I can even recall the little yellow flowers on the potholder I used for the icebox door so I could reach in and get the milk for my cornflakes.

1981

Truth to tell, I might've done one or two things different. I'm not saying a thing in this world against any of them, don't misunderstand me, I'm just saying about how you kindly like to do things your own way, that's just natural in a human. And then besides that, if I do say so, I know a little bit about these funerals. Buried my whole entire family at one time or another, that's every one of my nine brothers and sisters except Orphalee and Bertha, plus my mama and daddy of course, long years back, and my own firstborn son. Buried Carl Dee when he wasn't but fifty-two years old and I'll tell you something, when it's your own flesh and blood dies out of turn like that, well now you're just into something, that's all. But Carl Dee, he'd been knowing for a good little while he was on his way to meet his Maker so there was plenty opportunity for him to get things just like he'd like 'em, but with me, well, I woke up feeling sickly one morning and before the day was out, blam, I was dead. Wasn't much opportunity for planning things after that.

No, now, here's what I mean to say. Well, in the first place everybody got so scattered, nobody was seeing about Jo. They was seeing about her, but not the way I would've done it is what I'm saying. Oh, she just looked so pretty. Said she didn't feel pretty. All the folks kept coming in—Lord, you wouldn't have believed how many folks come in that house. Now, that's something I'm proud about, I will say that, they was lots of folks there, more than at Earl Tommy Stringer's even, I believe, but don't let me get off my story. The folks kept coming in, see, and one or two of them would say to Jo, well, you just look so pretty. But she just set there in her chair, said, "I don't feel pretty." She looked it though, now I'm here to tell you she did.

But they wouldn't see about her. Oh, Son tried and all, and

Orphalee and Bertha acted about her the same as they would've their own sister, always did, but they just wasn't capable of doing it the way I done it. Kindly hovered around on the couch, the both of 'em, Orphalee and Bertha, kept asking Jo if she needed anything. But those two poor old things, they're getting on up there themselves, you know. Bertha can't hardly hear now, nor walk neither, and Orphalee's in pretty close to the same shape. Just hobbles around like she's about half crippled. If Jo *had* needed anything I don't reckon they could've heard her, and if they did hear her I don't know how they could've got up and got it for her. Getting hard of hearing's an Alford trait I guess—about half the family's wound up with it at one time or another. And that leg business, now I don't know what causes that. Circulation or something. 'Course now, I was getting so's I couldn't hardly get around myself, just there towards the end. Might be it's another one of these inheritances, these old Alford traits. Oh, we had a lot of them. Characteristics, you might call 'em. Well, like with any family.

But now don't get me wrong, I know there's nobody can look after your own wife the way you could, I don't mean that. What I'm getting at here, I'm saying I wouldn't have minded if they'd all maybe paid a little less attention to getting the ceremonies just right and paid a little more attention to Jo.

She set quiet as a stone right there in that chair the whole morning long. Come time to get ready to go to the funeral, she pulled herself up out of it and headed out to the porch and down the steps the same as if she could see plain as anybody. Not a soul in this world helped her. Jo's eyesight's gone bad on her. Her corneas and such are deteriorating, these doctors down at Woolerton said. I don't know if that's a Lovitt trait or not, none of them ever lived long enough to find out.

Now, that's something strange. Jo was saying to somebody at the house there, oh, just a day or two after I died, about how she never expected to outlive me. Well, I sure never expected it nei-

ther. Oh, your statistics'll tell you about how the wife will generally outlive the man and all, but I don't know, those Lovitts,
seem like the majority of them just died off before they'd hardly
got to live their lives out, you might say. Lost her daddy when
she was just a girl. Flu. Caught it from fiddling on the porch,
near as I can recollect. And her mama died a young woman.
Didn't seem like it at the time, but now I look back on it I can
see how young she was. Heart attackt. And Jo, boy, I nearly lost
her two or three times. She had a bad heart too, don't you know.
Bad kidneys. Had to take medicine six times a day for all kind of
various things. But she just kept on coming back. 'Course, I had
a thing or two to do with that maybe, the way I looked after her
and all. But she always was a strong woman. Not what you'd call
strong in her organs necessarily, but strong in her mind. Strong-
willed. Mighty, mighty strong-willed woman. But, well, what with
her bad heart and her family history and all, I sure never did
expect her to outlive me.

And wouldn't you know it—that's what finally got me. Heart
attackt. Isn't that something? Life's odd. *I* never had no heart
trouble. That was on Jo's side of the family. But sure enough, it
did. I remember Son's in-laws coming to the funeral home. Mozelle's sister and her girl. Well, they'd had so much cancer and
all. In the family, you know. 'Course, now I had that too, I know
about this cancer business. But the doctors down at McAlester
cut on me and give me these cobalt treatments and I guess kept
it from getting any kind of a serious toehold, you know what I
mean, and I do thank the good Lord I didn't have to go that way.
But these folks was looking at me laying there so peaceful and
they says, "Mr. Alford looks so peaceful, don't he?"

Well, they knew. I guess they knew. Wasn't no more trouble
than laying down to sleep. Less. Oh, I was pretty sick there for
a while, let me tell you, I's a pretty sick man. But there towards
the end it was just as easy. The good Lord come to me, the Lord
Jesus I mean, and He says, "Now, Mr. Alford"—'course He knew

me, we'd been friends for years and years—"Mr. Alford," He says, "what-all have you done with your life?"

Well, I kindly looked around. I wasn't expecting Him, see. I was just laying there in the hospital bed with them tubes sticking around all over everwhere, plugged in any old place, now I mean you never saw the like. 'Course, by the time the Lord got there I was already out on one of these whadyacallems, these little shiny cords that strings you out from your body so's you can recognize the Lord and whoever else is on the other side that's come to see you, so I wasn't paying much attention to those tubes by that point. Look up in the corner, there's Carl Dee. Didn't say a word, just kindly hovered up there next to the ceiling—maybe They don't allow you to talk to them that's getting ready to come over, I don't know—but he had a big smile on his face and I hadn't seen one of them in a long, long time.

So the Lord asks me this question. I'm looking around. I look down at Son. He's sitting there so quiet and stiff. Praying most likely, or maybe just sitting, I don't know. He looked so tired. I tell you it's a strange thing when you look at your own son and he looks to you to be an old man. That ought to tell a body something right there, sign it's high time to move on out and make way for the young ones. Not that Son is what you'd call an old man, he's just gray-headed and wrinkled and about half bald and all. 'Course, all us Alfords is bald, that's another one of these characteristics I'm talking about. Couldn't ever a one of us seem to get grown, us Alford men, without our foreheads'd be shining clean to the back of our skulls. It's in the genes I expect.

But anyhow, there I was strung out on this shimmery do-bob, and here's my two sons, my two only-begotten in this world. The oldest one's floating around up by the ceiling looking like I always remember him, the way he looked in his absolute prime, like the very core of hisself, and now here's the other one, the baby, sitting there in a chair looking older than I ever felt or admitted to in my life. It's a weird feeling, I tell you. And I was trying to think how to answer the Lord.

Well, here's another thing that's a real mystery to me. They always say about how your whole life flashes before your eyes, but don't you believe it. The Lord asked me this question, see, and I couldn't no more answer Him than the man in the moon. My life didn't flash before my eyes, I had to get in there and go back over it piece by piece and *dig.* Same as if you was mining coal. Leastways the way it come to me that's so. I can't verify how it would be if a body died sudden, in a tornado, say, or a mine collapse. I've seen plenty men die sudden in these mines around here, back in the old days, but you know the living never have an inkling about what's going on with the dying. My, I've hauled them out of there burnt up with gas and everything else. I've seen a lot of 'em. Eyes open to the daylight.

No, but here's what I mean. People that dies sudden in any kind of mine accident or car wreck or what have you, it might be true that old saying about how their lives flash before their eyes—they's a lot of truth to some of these old sayings, that's one thing I've found out—but with me in this situation here, well, I was expecting and I wasn't expecting, you might say. They was plenty of time for any amount of digging and thinking and turning it over so I could answer the Lord. Turned out to be a lot of work, too.

Well sir, I started going back over my life. The good and the bad that I done. I'm shamed to tell it, but they was a lot of years in there I would've just as soon not remember. I didn't much like looking at myself rolling home drunk and hollering at Jo, that was an awful bad habit of mine at one time. 'Course, the fact is you don't get much choice about what you'd just as soon re-member. There wasn't any flashing going on, that's true, but here it all was anyhow, reeling itself out like a picture show from beginning to end. I'll admit I tried to go off the track.

I looked up at the Lord—He didn't look the least bit like I always pictured Him to, but of course I knew who He was anyhow—and I said, "Well, Mr. Jesus, I mined coal a good many years, 'course you knew that. Worked carpentry some, ran that Sinclair station awhile. Finally went into the mercantile business in fifty-nine, I guess it was, me and Jo opened up our little store down here on Main Street." But the Lord wasn't interested in what I worked at for a living, that wasn't what he was asking about and I knew it.

He just kept hanging there, humming around, glimmering. So I studied on it, turned things over, did a serious amount of considering. Afterwhile I said, "Lord, I'll have to admit looks to me like I have committed enough sins of o-mission and co-mission to send any sinner to hell if it wasn't for a merciful Jesus."

Jesus kindly winked at me then, you know, blinking His lights at me so to speak. He said, "You was some rapscallion, wasn't you?"

Well, I laughed right out loud, seemed like Son ought to hear me. But he just set there looking at the floor, holding everything inside him like he always done. Well, I looked back at the Lord then, said, "Yes sir, now Lord, I'll admit to it. You know me inside and out, wouldn't be any use to deny it. I did some bad and I did some good. But I always believed in You. I believed in doing right by my family and right by the other fellow, even where somehow or another I might've failed to do it."

Well, He kindly smiled then. Nearest you could claim a shining light could smile. But I knew what He was doing, we've been friends a mighty long time. Said, "Mr. Alford, now they was a lot of years in there."

"Eighty years, eleven months, and three hundred fifty-two days," is how I answered Him. 'Course, I knew by then I was coming on over to the other side and they wasn't no bargaining about it to be had. He said, "Yes, yes," and then it was kindly like He was thinking.

Now, this is another thing that's real curious to me. They's thousands of people dies every day, Christian people. And the good Lord has got time to be with every one of them, even if they're all dying at the same minute I guess. And He's got time to do the kind of figuring and probing and leaning on a fellow like I'm talking about here. I can't figure it out, the way He manages to be in all those places at once. The Lord does work in mysterious ways His wonders to perform, that's one old saying I've found out is true.

Well, He still didn't say anything. I figured I better do some more studying and hurry up about it. Not that I was afraid They wasn't going to let me in, you understand, but I don't know, you find out one thing is so different from what you always heard— I mean about Jesus not looking like His pictures—you start in to wondering if maybe there's other facts might turn out to surprise you. You begin to wonder what these questions are *for*. So I studied on it some more, dug around some, looked at what-all I'd done.

Finally I said, "Mr. Jesus, I want You to know something here, I was doing the best way I knew how to do. You ask me what I've done with my life and I don't know how to begin to answer You. *I* don't know what it was all about. I loved You, and I loved my wife and family. I worked hard from start to finish, raised up my sons in the way they should go like the Bible says, supported all of them the best I knew how. I never charged a nickel over what ought to have been charged in my store, never cheated on my taxes nor anything of the like. I never set out to hurt one person in this world. It's true I strayed from the path more times than I like to remember. I know I did my shameful share of drinking and carousing, know I probably ought to have done better on a lot of accounts. But I tried to follow what the Bible and the preacher and my own insides told me to do. That's all I know."

Jesus rose up then, smiling, blinking His lights, colors flying all over creation. Jesus said, "Mr. Alford"—oh, seemed like He was just radiating all over that room—"Mr. Alford," He says, "come on over Here."

Well, they wasn't no question about it. Good Lord knows when it's time, and then it's time. Didn't seem like I had anything to do with it, I don't guess a body ever does. Jesus called me, and I come.

But I'm getting sidetracked off my story.

I'd set out to tell you about the funeral, hadn't I?

Well, what I'm driving at, my main concern, see, was Jo. That's the main thing I would've done different—oh, they's one or two other little things maybe—but see now, here's your problem: the way I would've done things different would've pretty much flat required me to be there, in the flesh so to speak, and then of course you'd wind up with no purpose for the funeral at all. You can't compete with these paradoxes of life.

It was having to watch her, I think, gave me the most trouble. She looked so still and quiet and—and frail, sitting there in her chair. Made my heart ache to see it, and then to look over and see my own chair pulled up right next to hers, same as always, but just . . . empty. That house was full of people, not a one of them would sit in my chair. I don't blame 'em. They's something kindly spooky about the personal property of somebody that's just died. But it's like that just accented it, you know, the fact I was gone. I'd looked after her so careful for sixty-three years, this past dozen or so in particular after she took so sick that time and I come close to losing her, and then her eyes started going bad. I just kept a close watch on her all the time. Now, here, come time when I'd like to stand by her the most, why, I can't reach her. It's a mighty frustrating business, I can tell you. Then I look around at all the rest of them, they're running around like fire ants trying to make sure everything gets done right. And the only thing *I* care gets done right is for somebody to see about Jo. Isn't that the way of it?

Now I'm going to tell you something here. I don't know if They allow just everybody to hang around and look after things like They let me. Might be not all people that's passed on is privileged by the Lord to come look at their own funeral and see what-all their life was about. Might be sort of like a *re*ward, I don't know. I'm still studying on how They work things Here. But even if you get to look, you can't cross back over, and I don't guess anybody ever did except Jesus and Lazarus. That's the one all-time mystery. And those that's left behind, why, they don't know a thing. Their eyes are all veiled over. Through a glass darkly, just like the Bible says. See now, that's another one of these old sayings I've found out is true.

But there they were, all these folks with the scales of life, you might call it, pasted over their eyes, milling around in the yard, swarming inside the house, talking about who's going to ride in the family car with Jo and who's going to walk, who's going to drive out to the cemetery with so-and-so, who's going to do this-that-'n'-the-other. Son was wandering around hunting his girls. Seemed like he'd just get one of them rounded up and set still in one place and a different one would run off. 'Course, they're big old grown girls and there's not but three of them, but Son was getting all wound up over it, afraid they was going to be late for the funeral I guess. Well, I just laughed. *I* wasn't going nowhere. Son never could hold a rein on those girls when they was little, wasn't any use to start trying a half hour before the services was supposed to commence.

Don't get me wrong, they're good girls. They've got some kind of wild streak, I know—they might've took after me a little bit—but they're good girls. They'd just got back from the funeral home, see, and you could tell they was still pretty wound up. It was the first time they'd had a look at me dead in my coffin and you know that can be kindly perturbing to a young person's mind.

But the three of them, I tell you, if they're not a sight. They'd just drove in that morning, live all scattered off to Wichita and

Tulsa like most our young people anymore, and when they first
come in the room there at Seedly's they was just bawling like
babies. But then they got to fooling around. I guess Jo had give
them her Polaroid so she could get a picture of me in my coffin
for a last remembrance. We never could get through a Thanks-
giving dinner nor a Christmas without Jo would have to get her
a Polaroid snapshot of the food on the table or the packages on
the floor. Jo always liked to have her pictures of everything the
family done.

Well sir, after the girls had got through with their crying and
patting on me and calling me Papaw, they got ready to take this
picture. I knew Jo had put them up to it by the way they was
talking. They got to laughing about Grandma and her pictures
and moving flowers around to include them in the picture along
with me and the casket. And those girls got to giggling. Stuck
one of those long flowerdy things right in my face so it'd be sure
and be in the picture, and then they apologized: Sorry, Papaw!
Beg your pardon! Then they got to thinking how silly that was,
apologizing to a dead man, and they started giggling again. They
was laughing and crying and hugging each other, seemed like
they was whirlygigging all over that little room. Got so loud Mr.
Seedly had to come in once and shush 'em down. Then they
started trying to take the picture. One of them would step back
to take it, and I guess I'd just look pretty awful through the
viewfinder there, and she'd hand it over to her sister, say, "Here,
you do it." Then that one would look through the camera and
she'd get upset and giggly and hand it on and say, "*You* do it."

Finally ended up, Reba Jean took it. She's the baby. Said,
"There's nobody'd appreciate the humor in this more than Papaw." Now that's true. I always did have a good sense of humor,
loved to laugh and make jokes when I could. Well, I *was* laughing,
even if they didn't know it. But then the picture got to developing
and the girls would just look at it and put it down and look over
at each other, eyes big as saucers, shaking their heads. Say, "Oh

my Lord. This is awful. We can't show this to Grandma!" I reckon
you can't look any more dead than you do in a Polaroid snapshot
of yourself laying in your coffin.

But now how'd I get way off on that?

Well, yes, here was Son trying to round up his girls. Wanting
to start that funeral right on the nose I reckon, but I don't know
what difference it made. Didn't make none to me and I's what
you might call the guest of honor. But see, that's what I'm talking
about. They was so worried about getting it right, seemed like
everybody forgot about Jo. She just set there in her chair no
bigger-looking than a songbird till Son come told her it was time.
Up she got then, just pulled herself up and headed out the door,
every bit alone.

Lord, she looked so . . . frail, I don't know how to explain it,
coming down those front steps. I'll tell you something, that's the
hardest part about this dying business—having to watch them
that's still behind the veil and how they're grieving and sorrowing
for you, and you can't do a thing in the world to comfort them.
I wouldn't have changed it, I wouldn't have not *been* there, but
it like to broke my heart, now, that's all.

But Son caught up to his mother there at the foot of the steps
and took her arm and helped her on out to that long black car.
See, now I never should've said a word about it. He was doing
the best he knew how. Naturally he can't look after her the same
way as me, he don't know all her little quirks and all. But he
always was awful good to his mother, both my boys was. 'Course,
I learnt 'em that when they was just little.

Well, they loaded up in that big black thing, Son helped his
mother, the three girls helped Bertha and Orphalee, Son's wife
Mozelle supervised the arrangements, and the bunch of 'em drove
around the block while the rest of the folks walked the measly
hundred yards across the street from the house to the church.

Now, that's one little thing I might've done different. Jo and
me walked across that street every Sunday morning for sixty-

three years. Didn't seem right somehow seeing her get in that big old black limousine and circle around the block to get there. I know they give it to you in a package there at the funeral home and all so you don't like to turn it down, and I know Son and them wanted to do it up right, I'm not complaining, you understand. Just seemed to me strange.

I will say one thing though, now this is something that made my heart glad: they was a mighty number of folks in that church sanctuary. Had to set up chairs in the back. Made me just pretty proud, I can tell you. I lived right here in this community my whole life and I guess I made myself a friend or two, they said I did anyhow, and folks turned out for my funeral, I'll say that for 'em. Come from all over this county. And Lord at the flowers. You never saw the like of flowers in your life. Whole altar was filled near to overflowing. Election board even sent a spray— 'course, I worked on the election board for years and years. Now, that sort of thing is what I meant about getting to see what your life was about. Spend your whole life trying to do right by the other fellow and comes to the end you find out just how much they all appreciate it. That's the best part of anybody's funeral.

Not that folks around here don't always turn out good for funerals. They do. That's one thing, if you live and die around Cedar you're bound to have a churchful of mourners at your funeral whether you like it or not, and even sour old man Waters had the whole Church of Christ filled up at his and they wasn't a thing he could do by that point to run 'em off. Well, partly I think it's because our population's so old—over half the town qualifies for lunch at the Senior Citizens and the young ones have all moved off—I don't reckon anybody wants to take a chance on not showing up for somebody else's funeral in case they wind up with a poor showing at their own. And then again, these ladies at the church always put out a really fine spread of food in the fellowship hall after the services, so that might contribute to the big turnout too, but in my particular situation here, that church

was more crowded than I believe I'd seen it in a long time. Folks
had come from all over this county and half the state—even had
one cousin showed up all the way from Prescott, Arizona—and
that church was full well jam-packed.

Well, the family come in last, of course, and filed into the front
pews, and they went ahead and commenced.

First off the music minister and his little wife stood up and
sang "How Great Thou Art." That must've been Jo's idea. She
knew how much I loved that hymn. I always did love to sing that
hymn. Well, it just rang to the rafters the way Brother and Miz
Akins sang it. Me here on the other side, I couldn't help pondering
how I used to think I knew what Great was and how the truth
is I didn't know but about a fingernail's worth, but that hymn
touched it, come mighty close to touching it. Wasn't a dry eye
in the place time it was over. Moved me so much I had to say
amen, but of course nobody could hear me.

Now, if I'd just thought beforehand I would've told somebody
to make my funeral long on the singing and short on the preach-
ing. That's one little thing I would've changed. You can't send a
body to heaven any truer way than making a joyful noise unto
the Lord, like the Bible says, because there's things a hymn'll
tell you that no sermon will. But this one hymn's all they had by
way of music, and then they went on.

Joe Bledsoe stood up and said a few words about my life and
all. Said how he'd always knew me as a friend. Well sir, now
that's true. I always did have a lot of friends. But Lord how that
made them on the front rows bawl, almost made me wisht he
hadn't said it. And then Brother Packer got up to preach his
sermon.

It was a beautiful sermon, it really was, about how I was still
living Here on the other side in the bosom of Jesus, and how we
could all meet again in Glory if only we was saved. Well, I hoped
it made everybody's heart glad, because I knew it was true and
I was glad to be living in the bosom of Jesus, but I don't know

. . . Brother Packer went ahead and commenced to try and save everybody there at the church. Well, that didn't seem quite fitting to me, seeing as how about half the congregation was already members there at First Baptist anyhow.

I'll tell you something else—'course, I didn't know this when I was on the other side and I know they don't know it either— but They're a lot more lenient Here than I ever thought. Surprised me when I saw some of these Catholic I-talians I'd mined coal with down at Hughes hanging around when I first come over. But afterwhile you start getting used to them being around and start seeing how if They didn't let none but the Baptists—or none but the Baptists and the Church of Christs, say—come in, why, that'd leave a terrible number of lost souls crying around for eternity, and leave it be a little lonesome Here besides.

What I mean is, I might just as soon the preacher'd preached about the love of God and the bosom of Jesus and left off trying to save everybody in favor of more music. I'll swan if I didn't think he was going to give an invitation before it was all over. I'm not faulting Brother Packer, he's a good man, a fine man, one of the best there is and helped my own family through many a trial and sickness. That's just how he believes and all, like a lot of 'em. I'm just mentioning how if I'd had any say-so in the matter.

But they went ahead and wrapped her up then. Everybody filed down front to pay their last respects. I was glad they did that, opened the coffin up there at the altar and let everybody come by so the family could see who all'd showed up. They've quit doing that, last few funerals I've went to. These funeral directors have taken to wheeling the casket out back while everybody's head's bowed in prayer so folks can pass by on their way out the door, but the family never does get to know who all was there. They're sitting up front you know, and nobody wants to go cran- ing their neck around at a time like that.

Took a good half hour to get through it. 'Course, they don't hardly look at you much anyhow, they scoot by pretty fast—folks don't much like looking at dead people—but they was just so many. They was folks there I'd do business with about every day of my life and folks I hadn't seen in twenty years. Seemed a real shame I couldn't mingle around and visit with them, they was a lot of 'em I'd liked to had a good long visit with. I always was what you might call a sociable creature, always did love to visit around with people. But now I don't know why it is that folks'll travel hundreds of miles to attend a person's funeral when they never came to see him still living. It's a shame. I'll admit to the fact I did it myself, but that don't keep it from being a terrible shame.

Last of all, of course, come the family. I couldn't imagine how it had shrunk up so small. When I was a boy I had kinfolks all over this county, I'm talking about near kin, and now here, come to the end of it, my family'd shrunk up to this one little handful. And Jo and Orphalee and Bertha—well, Son too, come to speak of it—they all looked pretty shrunk up themselves. Seemed to me like the whole world had got small. Nothing seemed like it amounted to more than a driblet. The same as my family, same as this shrinking town here. Same as the tiny-boned size of my wife.

They come by real slow. Some of 'em was crying pretty hard, especially the girls. And they each one said their goodbye. And I heard 'em. I guess the Lord privileged me to do that, or it may be anybody can hear what's thought and murmured and whispered over their coffin. I don't know. It's not given to me to know everything yet. They prayed, some of them. Goodbye, they every one whispered. I loved you, Papaw. I loved you, Allie. I loved you, Dad.

But now here's the strange thing, the glorious thing. I don't know how They arrange this—it's kindly like the Lord being at every body's passing maybe, the same principle as that—but I somehow or another had an experience with every one of those loved ones. When Bertha hobbled by, why, there was our whole life together, brother and sister, from the beginning, back yonder as kids, and even back before that. I knew what we were to one another. You can't explain this in words. But there it was flowing back and forth between us. Just then. And here come Orphalee. Same thing.

Well, you think you understand who you are—brother, father, grandfather, husband—but you don't in this life. Not really. You can't. At the end, though, They see to it you get to know it in the fullness of it. The truth of a whole lifetime, how another's life and yours fit together, all of it passing by in the twinkling of an eye, like the Book says. What each one of those humans was to you. What you were to them. Individual. Private. Just exactly between you and them.

Jo was the last to come forward of course, that's how these funeral directors always direct it. Mr. Seedly hisself had her by the arm.

It's strange, you know. I was still communing with Son, still passing that understanding that passeth understanding back and forth between us. I sort of had to make myself look over and see Jo. And I thought to myself, My, she just looks so little and blind and . . . old. How'd we get so old? She looked mighty far away from me then.

I floated there thinking that a person just can't believe how fast this little scrap of life we've been bequeathed slips away. You start out in it, you think you've got all the time in the world. I married her when she was fifteen years old. Wasn't but seventeen myself. Mining coal. Oh, we thought we was grown up, sure, but we was just babies. Sixty-three years. Still, there wasn't near time enough.

Jo reached me then, or reached that old shell of me.

Well, and now here's the last thing.

Jo stood there crying. But soft, you know. She kept ahold of herself real well. Mighty strong-willed woman, like I said. And I could see her then. I knew her. She wasn't any shrunk-up, hunched-over blind woman. She was Jo. This woman I'd gone through every mile of my life with since both of us was teenagers, the one bore my sons, slept with me and didn't sleep with me, talked to me and didn't talk to me, fought with me and depended on me and kicked me out on my ear two or three times, the one knew me inside and out, better than any living soul, I reckon, excepting the very Lord Hisself. And Jo stood there, patting my hands.

I felt just what my hands felt like to her in that moment. I knew how cold and hard and smooth they were under her hands. I remembered how the first time I saw my daddy dead, laid out in the parlor, way back there, how I expected him at any moment to just sit up. I remembered how for years after he was gone I used to dream that he did that, sat up in his coffin, how I thought the same thing when I looked at poor dead Carl Dee. And now here Jo stood patting me. For all that woman's faith, all her knowledge of death, she couldn't anymore believe I was gone than I believed it of my daddy a half century ago. People, I think, just somehow never can.

But now here's the truth of things:

If I could've gone back right then, I would have.

Knowing all that I know now—and I never was afraid of dying, never afraid for a moment from that first flash I caught of the Lord—and knowing I'd be going back to old aches and pains and a body that couldn't hardly get around anymore, understanding fully I'd have to be returning to sorrow and sickness and maybe a long slow awful way of dying, I still would've slipped back along that gossamer strand, if Anybody'd allowed it, slipped back into that old body. Just to be there with Jo.

That's one thing I would've done.

'Course, it's a good thing They don't allow it, I can see that. They've got good reasons for how They work things Here, They've studied all this out. They know just how humans are. If I'd got back to my body and sat up in my coffin, why, that sure enough would've give Jo a heart attackt, and about half the other mourners besides. And there Jo and me would've wound up on opposite sides of the veil anyhow. We might could've spent Eternity chasing each other, flipping back and forth.

So there wasn't any alternative but for Jo to just stand there beside my empty shell in the final moments of my funeral. She stayed there a good long time before they closed the lid of that coffin. Whispering to me. Patting my hands.

1983

D.H. DeWitt had a dozen or more tricks he could pull with a rattlesnake, but his pure favorite was walking into a bar with one curled up under his hat. He liked to saunter in slow and take a long look around before he eased over to the bar and ordered himself a shot of Wild Turkey and a draw. He'd pour the whiskey into the beer, turn around to face the room with his elbows propped behind him, and locate just the right patron to engage in a conversation. Generally he preferred if it was a woman, and he preferred it even better if she was good-looking, but any old cowboy ugly as a stump would do so long as it was a stranger. When D.H. had the other party off guard and least suspecting, he'd say something like, "Mighty warm in here, ain't it? I'm about to burn up," and act like he was going to wipe the sweat off his forehead. The captured instant when D.H. whisked off his hat and the stranger spied that fat rattlesnake curled up and drowsy on top of his head was the high point of D.H.'s existence.

He could do other things with a snake, would casually wrap one around his fist and wear it like a bracelet or dangle a five-footer by the tail end with its head writhing free so that anyone who didn't have D.H.'s quick reflexes would have been bit in a second, but the DeWitt hat trick was the one that fulfilled him. There was something about the surprise in it that touched D.H.'s soul.

If the witness was a woman and if she screamed and jumped back and started carrying on and shouting, D.H. generally laughed, but then sometimes he'd wind up apologizing and would take the snake outside and put it back in the sack on the floorboard of his truck. If it was a man and if the man tried to act big-assed by not saying a word, D.H. generally kept on talking and after a while nonchalantly put his hat back on his head, leaving the man to wake up the next morning wondering if he hadn't better slow down some on drinking. If the man made a comment as to the fact that D.H. had a snake on his head, D.H. would reach up with one hand and grab the snake just behind the eyes and pull it down, staring at it in amazement like he couldn't begin to figure how such a thing got up there. Often as not, D.H. got thrown out of the bars where he pulled his hat trick, but there were plenty of bars and honky-tonks all over the hills of southeastern Oklahoma and he would travel as far as Broken Bow or Antlers on a weekend in order to find a good place to drink where nobody knew him.

On weeknights D.H. stuck closer to home. Cedar, of course, didn't have a sign of a bar, never had had one from time immemorial and most likely never would on account of liquor being considered by the predominant Baptists to be Satan's own elixir, but D.H., like any other drinking man in town, was used to having to drive a ways to do his drinking. He'd take off after work down to the High Life near Talihina, eat boiled eggs and Slim Jims for supper and wash them down with boilermakers. The old boys there all knew him, so D.H. had to content himself with only talking about snake hunting, but he liked to make sure he had a half dozen good-sized rattlers in his truck in a sack in case some smartassed stranger happened in and didn't believe him that he could stick his hand in there and pull one of those suckers out headfirst and never once get bit.

But one sultry June Monday evening D.H. found his pickup heading west instead of south when he turned onto the highway after work at the Arkhoma gas well. It was either the heat or the humidity or else that fool Carston Kramer, who'd told him Friday night that if he ever caught him wagging another rattlesnake into the High Life again he'd personally tie it in a bow knot around D.H.'s neck and stuff the business end down his fool braggerty throat. Whyever it was, D.H. didn't feel much like going to Talihina, and by the end of happy hour he'd made a pit stop at Pete's Place in Woolerton, had cruised through the Pioneer in Harts-horne, downed several two-fers at the Black Saddle in Haileyville, and was sitting half-crocked and happy at a little round table near the dance floor in the dark downstairs lounge at the McAlester Holiday Inn.

That's when Verlita walked in.

D.H. hadn't seen her in seventeen and a half years, but he recognized her immediately. She looked just the same, only older and a bit softer around the middle, and blond now. But the easy way she moved across the floor, like she was floating past all the eyes of the world and didn't care to look back at a one of them, was just the same. And the way she leaned over the bar for a light, reaching out to steady the bartender's hand when he held up the lit match, was a movement seared into D.H.'s brain by countless repetitions of memory and dream. He'd only seen her do that one time, but it had been his own shaking hand holding the match, and the place where she'd touched had burned hot for days. They'd been standing in the dark on the main street of Cedar. Verlita had been waiting for D.H.'s big brother Larry to come out of the pool hall. D.H. had been fifteen years old.

"Verlita McHenry," D.H. said softly to himself, and then just sat with his fist around his beer glass, shaking his head, as if that said it all.

Two fellows who'd been drinking quietly and separately all evening suddenly got friendly with each other, talking in loud voices, insulting each other and horsing around, but Verlita paid them no attention. She sat staring into the mirror behind the bar, blowing out smoke through her nostrils. The lounge was mostly empty, one old drunk mumbling to himself at a table, a man and woman necking in the far back corner, the two cowboys at the bar. And D.H.

I believe I'll just step up there and say hi, D.H. thought. But the whiskey and beer running through his veins made his boots feel suddenly huge and hard and clumsy, made his mouth feel mushy, his tongue swollen and lazy, even while the top of his brain was blowing off firecrackers, sharp and crackling, quick, full of pretty words and sudden deep insights. D.H. was amazed at his own ability to see the connections in things, the way life was all one big circle, or a web, and every soul in it connected by invisible threads. Just like Verlita McHenry walking in here to the lounge at the Holiday Inn. Just like that. And on a Monday, too. And on any other Monday of the world, D.H. DeWitt would be sitting at the High Life in Talihina and never know that Verlita McHenry was at that moment sitting in the lounge at the Holiday Inn. In McAlester. D.H. shook his head at the amazing way life had of unfolding in front of a person. He shook it again to try and clear it some. Then he took another drink to see if that wouldn't help. At last he decided he'd get up and go take a leak so that maybe when he got back his tongue would be thinner.

A few more customers had come in by the time D.H. sat back down, all of them male and all of them crowded around the bar where Verlita still sat staring at the mirror like she was alone in the room. Ricky Skaggs was singing on the jukebox. The noise level bouncing around the red-and-gold flocked walls far outstripped the number of people on account of all the men talking loud and self-conscious, but for all the acknowledgment she made, Verlita might as well have been stone deaf.

I believe I'll just step up there and ask her to dance, D.H. thought, and waited for his boots to carry him. He sat gazing at Verlita, thinking how her eyes would go wide with surprise once she'd recognized him. She might even throw her arms around him to hug his neck after all these years. Right in front of that whole damn crew of loud-talking men. D.H. saw himself guide her onto the dance floor with his hand at the small of her back. He'd tell her what-all Larry'd been up to for seventeen and a half years in case she was interested, coaching ball down at Stigler and winning state four years back and the divorce and all. He might let drop a few of his own accomplishments, in particular the fact he'd won damn near every prize there was to win at the annual rattlesnake roundup at Okeene last year. He could see those loudmouthed cowboys at the bar glaring at the two of them while he guided her smoothly around the floor.

Still, D.H.'s boots didn't make any kind of move to untangle themselves from beneath the table and carry him to the bar. Welp, D.H. thought, filling his cheeks with air, blowing out a long steady stream, looks like I'm about ready for a beer. Reckon I'll have to step up there and order it. Reckon it's not going to come over here and plop down on my table of its own accord.

That did the trick, and in a moment D.H. was standing over Verlita's shoulder, carefully not looking at Verlita or her face in the mirror while the bartender drew the beer. D.H. left off the shot of Wild Turkey this time.

He drank down the draft and motioned for another, and before he had time to stop himself, got up the gumption to tap her lightly on the arm. Slowly her eyes turned away from the mirror and traveled up to D.H.'s face. He waited for her to say something, waited for it to come clear to her who he was, but no flicker of recognition crossed her face.

D.H. was stumped. He'd thought sure she would know him. He'd known her in a second, surely she was bound to know him. D.H. could feel his tongue swelling up, getting clumsy inside his mouth. He'd meant to call her by name, say, Verlita McHenry, how the hell are you, long time no see, but now he was afraid his fat tongue would give him away. Helpless, D.H. shrugged his shoulders once and tipped his hat at her and grinned. Verlita smiled and turned her eyes back to the mirror.

Not sure just what way to carry on from there, D.H. turned and commenced talking to the fellow standing next to him. The other fellow said how he'd just acquired the prettiest little feist squirrel dog from an old boy up around Okmulgee, was the truthfulest dog he ever knew anything about. If that dog so much as blinked at a tree, he said, there was damn sure a squirrel in it, you could bet your life on it, she'd never lied to him once. They proceeded from there to talk about hunting in general and squirrel hunting in particular, and from there the conversation just naturally turned to rattlesnakes.

D.H. didn't let on how he was the finest damn snake wrangler in the entire state of Oklahoma and had taken prizes at Okeene six years in a row—he figured this other old boy could figure it out for himself—but he did point out some of the more dangerous aspects of locating and live-capturing a full-grown western diamondback, the flat-out meanest, orneriest, quickest to rattle and fastest to strike of any creature God ever made to crawl on its belly.

"I'll have you know," D.H. told the squirrel hunter, "a rattler can't see worth a damn but it can strike in pitch dark. Did you know that? They got heat detectors, like these damn missiles, lets 'em know just where their target's at." D.H. inched up the volume just a tad. "They can whip out a full third their own length and strike a target dead-on and get back to coil so fast the human eye can't see it. Daylight or dark. That's a fact." Damned if D.H.'s tongue wasn't getting slicker and quicker all while he talked. He motioned the bartender to pour him a shot of Wild Turkey. "Not only that," he told the squirrel hunter, "did you know that a rattler's ability to kill with a minimum of bodily contact is only exceeded by man himself? That's true. Matter of fact, there's not hardly a more dangerous undertaking in the world than rounding up rattlesnakes, if you don't know what you're doing. The whole trick is, you got to know their nature. Got to know how to handle 'em once you've caught 'em, that's the thing."

He went on to describe for the squirrel hunter a few of the trickier tactics he'd developed, showed the man just what he was talking about with his hands, and meantime kept a secret surreptitious eye on Verlita's face in the mirror. She hardly blinked. But man she looked good. For an older woman, that is. And then D.H. started trying to figure just how old she'd be now. She'd been an older woman back then even, or seemed like it anyway. Hell, Larry was four years older than D.H., and Verlita McHenry had been older than him. But then D.H. kept figuring and it came to him that, still, all things considered, still, Verlita McHenry couldn't be much over forty, forty-one now.

D.H. felt himself relax. He tipped back his hat, rolled the base of the beer glass between his thumb and forefinger, caught a look at himself in the mirror. Forty wasn't so damn old. Hell, lots of thirty-two-year-old men went with forty-year-old women, probably. It wasn't unheard of. Hell, Sonny Lewman ran off to Texas with that Chuleewah woman and she was damn near old enough to be his grandmother.

Thus D.H. talked to himself, one eye on Verlita, the other on his own reflection in the mirror, and his mouth telling the squirrel hunter how most rattlers' bites wasn't no more worse than a flu shot if you took care of it right, he ought to know, he'd been bit seven times and never wound up in the hospital yet. But D.H. never could catch Verlita's eye. He could hear himself revving up louder and louder, but Verlita went on stirring her drink and smoking and sitting. Every time she pulled a Salem Light out of the white pack on the bar there was a mad scramble in the general vicinity while a half dozen pairs of hands fumbled for matches and lighters, but D.H. never managed to be first up with his.

This sorry pass might have continued till closing if the man on the far side of Verlita—who was fifty if he was a day and wearing a suit and a string tie, for godsake—hadn't asked her to dance. Verlita pushed herself back on the bar stool, stood, and headed across the room with that easy side-to-side sway, and stopped in the middle of the dance floor with her arms lifted, waiting for the old man to step in.

"I'll be go to hell," D.H. said, and the fellow with the new little feist said, "Old rats like cheese too, I reckon," and called for a shot of Jack Daniel's straight up.

D.H. watched them dancing, watched them stop when the song finished and the man lean down and say something, watched Verlita shake her head no and glide back over the stained red carpet and climb onto her stool.

"Mister," D.H. said, turning to the squirrel hunter, "you hold my place right here, right *here*, right in this place right here," making a great general sweep over his head with his arm. "Much obliged. Got to go see a man about a dog," and he walked out of the lounge and up the stairs to the parking lot. He took a leak on the right rear tire of a new Buick in the lot, then went to his truck and opened the passenger side door where the wheat-colored tote sack lay on the floorboard, and reached in.

When he came back into the lounge, Verlita and the squirrel hunter were dancing.

That's all right, D.H. told himself. That is just all right. That is plumb fine and dandy. He went to the bar and ordered a shot and a draw.

Leaning back on the bar with his elbows propped behind him, D.H. realized how drunk the room was. Drunk and smoky and noisy out of all proportion to the number of men there, and here Verlita was gliding around like she didn't have an idea in the world what she was doing to them all. D.H. could feel anger rising inside him. He ordered another setup of Wild Turkey and beer. When Verlita came back with the squirrel hunter, D.H. took her by the elbow without saying a word and whirled her around and pushed her back out to the dance floor. She went with him smooth as slow-moving water and lifted her arms for him to step in.

But when D.H. slipped his hand around Verlita's waist, drew her to him and felt the soft roll of skin and muscle and the sweet little ridge of fat over her waistband, his anger let go at once and fell clean away. He slid his palm up along her blouse so that his thumb rested just against the curve of her breast. Lord, he thought, lord, lord, lord, lord. He felt himself back fifteen years old again and a virgin, putting himself to sleep at night with his hands under the covers, dreaming of what Larry and Verlita looked like naked in the back seat of Larry's old Dodge. Despite the powerful amount of liquor he'd had, D.H. felt himself rising against her. That pleased him. I bet there's not that many damn men in this country, he thought, can drink a quart of whiskey and wash it down with half a keg of beer and slow-dance a white woman in one evening with a full-fledged hard-on and a three-foot rattler under his hat.

The snake was uneasy. D.H. could feel the tenseness of its underbelly coiled against his scalp. This one was too big for the space and D.H. knew it, and mean from the heat, but the rattler's uneasiness didn't bother him, seemed like it just made him more excited, and he let go of Verlita's hand wedged between them, reached around with both palms pressed against the muscles at the tops of her hips, pulled her hard against him. He mumbled into her hair, smelling the hairspray and cigarettes, "It's been a helluva long time."

Verlita pulled back and looked up at him. He expected in that moment for it to dawn on her, but she only looked at him, flat-faced, curious. D.H. stopped still in the middle of the dance floor, waiting. He wanted her to come to it on her own without him having to say it. Finally something like a glimmer, not of recognition but of comprehension, passed over Verlita's face. She smiled a knowing little smile at him, amused, shaking her head. "You don't say," she said.

It was then that D.H. realized that she wasn't going to know him. She might not remember him even if he told the whole story, said remember that old boy from around Cedar you used to go with, remember old Larry DeWitt, District Basketball Champion 1966, remember his little shrimp of a brother? D.H. felt himself small, the way he'd been back then, no more worth her notice than a speck on the wall.

"You got a name?" Verlita said. The top half of her body was still pulled away, her fingers lightly touching his shoulders, hips retreating inside his hands. But she kept on looking square at him, with that little half smile on her face.

"You got one?"

"No, come on now, don't do that. What's your name?"

D.H. looked at her a minute, then he tightened his hands around her and pulled her in close again, pressed the side of his chin to the side of her head. It was no good to tell her. He didn't want to just come out and tell her. It'd be too much like getting beat at foosball or poker, too much like losing somehow.

He thought about making her guess. He could say, Verlita McHenry, I know you but you don't recognize me. I know you was born and raised over at Heavener, your daddy hauled cattle for J.D. Wilkerson for God knows how many years, you're a natural-born redhead underneath that blond hair and the middle toes on both your feet hooks over the big one and you wear a size 36-C brassiere, or anyhow did, and you left Heavener and moved to Bakersfield, California, in 1968. Now think back a minute and see if you can't guess who this old boy is standing here talking to you. If you want I'll give you a hint.

But D.H. couldn't bring himself to say it. To tell the truth, it was bad enough she didn't recognize him. He just didn't want to hear it if, as he secretly suspected, it turned out she couldn't remember that a D.H. DeWitt had ever existed once he'd pointed it out.

All at once D.H. took in a long breath. Over Verlita's shoulder where she couldn't see, he began to swallow deep and wiggle his tongue inside his mouth. He opened his eyes wide and blinked them a few times, pressed his lips tight together, opened them, stretched them wide, opened and closed his mouth, opened and closed his eyes. He could do it sometimes, could get himself very near sober by a clean act of will, just by concentrating hard enough, giving himself the right juice. D.H. shook himself around a little, pressed his thighs against her, and picked up the dancing pace. It had just occurred to him that he could invent himself for Verlita, could tell any kind of story he wanted to tell, and she'd never know the difference. It was better even than a pure stranger, because he knew her history. And she didn't know his.

"The name's Hank," D.H. said, pulling back to look at Verlita, thinking, and not knowing he was thinking, of Hank Harriman Ryder, who'd left Cedar in '78 and gone on to make a high-powered rodeo star. "Hank Rogers," D.H. said, and lifted one hand to touch the brim of his hat. He heard, or sensed, through the top of his head a sound like a boot rustling through dry leaves. He slid his hands down and pulled her tighter against him with his palms cupped under her butt. It was beautiful the way her cheeks fit perfect inside the cups of his hands.

"Ride rodeo," he mumbled. Then he cleared his throat. "I bust broncs," he said, like he was answering a question, "Ride the circuit all around in these parts, Texas, Montana. Have done for years. You ever heard of me?"

Verlita shook her head.

"Hank Rogers." D.H. said the words slow and careful. "Hank Thomas Rogers. Junior." That "junior" tacked on there made it sound more real, but still Verlita shook her head.

That was all right. D.H. didn't mind that. Truth was, D.H. knew plenty of facts about most anything anybody'd ever want to know about, but rodeo riding didn't happen to be one of his areas of expertise. Still the image of himself as a rodeo star was really fine, and his head and other parts swelled with the idea.

"Bust broncs, do a little calf ropin', barrel ridin', what have you. Well. There's easier ways of making a living, ain't they?"

This last was said with a little shrug and a modest grin, but

when he glanced down he saw that Verlita wasn't even looking
at him. She was staring off over his shoulder with that same
dreamy look she'd had when she was staring into the mirror
behind the bar. Two fine little vertical lines curved on either side
of her mouth, and it seemed to D.H. that those lines were purely
the sexiest things he'd ever seen. He tightened his hands harder
around her rear end. "You got a sweet ass, you know that?" he
whispered in her ear.

Verlita moved her hand from his shoulder and put it against
his chest. She didn't say anything, didn't push back on him, but
just held it there flat and solid over his heart. D.H. felt his hands
go slack, the same as if she'd ordered it. He touched her lightly,
shuffling with the music. Then he pulled his head back to look
at her.

The bones in Verlita's face were perfectly still. Sometimes her
lips moved with the music, but the movement just served to show
how still her face was, and her eyes never changed. D.H. thought
there was a terrible sadness in that look. An uncomfortable feeling
passed over him, womanish, peculiar, and he felt like he wanted
to move his grabby hands away from her butt, wrap his arms
around her back, pull her to him and comfort her, soothe her,
stroke her head. D.H. fought the feeling. Last thing on earth he
intended to do was make a fool out of himself in front of Verlita.
In front of that crew of loud-talking men.

D.H. shook his head slightly and tightened his hold. He glanced
toward the bar where, he thought sure, the old man and the
squirrel hunter were watching them in the mirror. He looked
back down at Verlita. The sweeping spots of light from the mirror
ball flicked over her skin, and it seemed to him in that moment
that Verlita's face went hard. It wasn't like her expression
changed but like what was already there suddenly got set in
cement, and D.H. thought maybe it was the lights and then he
thought maybe it was the music because it was Patsy Cline singing about hurt me now, get it over, and then he thought, no, it

was just her, just the way women were. Hard like that when they wanted to be. A man could drop dead right in front of 'em and they'd just politely step over the corpse and go on.

D.H. smiled a little to himself, smiled at his own deep perceptions of the way women were. He knew how to handle women like that. He slid his hands down rough till his fingers jabbed each other in the crack where her cheeks met. He thrust his pelvis forward, moved to pull her hard against him, but even as he moved, Verlita stepped into him. She hugged up against him, touching him, mouthing Patsy Cline's words. A sudden helpless sensation sank over D.H., like he'd reached out to strike something with his fist and felt that something give way and turn to soft mush against his hand. Verlita's voice came into his ear, not sweet like Patsy's but with that same whine and break, like her heart was split open and never could be fixed. He held onto her. They moved around the floor pressed tight to the front of each other, D.H. moving exactly to Verlita's rhythm, like slow-moving water.

Man, D.H. thought. Man. This is something. He shut his eyes, feeling it, amazed at the way he and Verlita lined up true. Like faultless-cut seams. The way they fit together. Perfect. A perfect damn fit. He wondered at the mysterious way a woman's heighth was all in her legs. A man's heighth was in his trunk, and here was D.H., half a head taller than her, not so tall maybe but tall enough, and here the two of them fit together perfect—damned perfect—right where it counted, on account of Verlita's long legs. He knew then he'd lost some fitted part of himself a long time ago and just now found it. He'd always been meant to be with Verlita McHenry, he knew that. He couldn't have got away from her if he'd tried. D.H.'s heart swelled to match his other parts, and he hugged Verlita to his chest.

At once she whirled away from him.

D.H. stepped backwards as Merle Haggard's voice swung into the room, crowing about how he thought he was going to live forever, and Verlita pranced and sashayed all over the floor. D.H. wheeled around, dazed, looking for the bastard who'd punched that song in. The squirrel hunter had his back turned and the old man was gone. Nobody was standing at the jukebox. D.H. cursed once, and tried, but fast dancing was just something outside of his repertoire of things he could do right then, so he stood swaying side to side, half raising his arms and trying to snap his fingers while Verlita danced around him.

She was wild, twirling in circles, flinging her arms like there was something dirty at the ends of them she'd like to hurl across the room. D.H. could feel the rattler restless, writhing, trying to go someplace under his hat. Verlita was turned away from him, facing the mirrored tiles along the back wall. Her hips rotated in circles, her hands open, elbows stabbing the air. D.H. took a step toward her. She whirled around again, and D.H. saw her face, lips tight, eyes staring at nothing, but steady in the sliding light, concentrated and fierce.

D.H. knew then that it wasn't him. Not how he'd thought, like they were true matched seams. It could have been any man. He believed in that moment it could have been any man.

He stood still in the middle of the dance floor, dizzy, sick to his stomach from the flickering lights. He hated the ceaseless slow sweep, the spots of staccato white light flick-flashing across him, and he thought he'd like to lay down on the floor right then, just lay down and quit. The old hated paltriness crept over him, turning his insides ugly and small. Without thinking, he flashed into anger. Probably she was just a whore, no different from the rest of them. Pretending to want him. Pretending to be matched up to him. Rubbing against him with her 36-C's. She was a whore, sure she was, he'd known that all along. The rattler moved under his hat, not forward or sideways because it was curled up too tightly, but writhing on his scalp, rippling its powerful muscles, moving and motionless, caught in one place.

D.H. stepped back, turned, stepped sideways to catch his balance, and weaved his way across the carpet through the spindly black chairs and round tables toward the bar. He leaned heavily against the black naugahyde padding and ordered a double whiskey, downed it, motioned for another. In a moment he felt Verlita standing beside him.

"What's the big idea?" she said.

D.H. stood blinking at her. The shaded lights over the bar deepened the curved lines at the sides of her mouth, showed up tiny radiating cracks at the corners of her eyes, the softness of her jawline, the little place under her chin where the skin was starting to sag. D.H. saw all this, but still it didn't seem like he could see her. He couldn't put all the parts into a whole.

Verlita turned abruptly and sat on the bar stool and reached for a cigarette. The squirrel hunter came from behind D.H. to light it. D.H. watched them in the mirror as they started talking, but the music and the whiskey and the confusion in his brain kept him from comprehending a word that they said.

D.H. reached for Verlita's arm. "Listen," he said. There was something he meant to say. He couldn't get the words to formulate in his brain, or when he'd find them they'd slip away before he could pull them up front to his tongue.

"Listen," he said.

Verlita and the squirrel hunter looked at him.

"There's lives," D.H. said slowly, wagging a finger at them, "there's jus' certain kinds a lives."

Verlita and the squirrel hunter kept looking at him. Then they looked at each other, and Verlita gave a slight shrug with her shoulders. She said, "You got a name?" "Frank," the squirrel hunter said, and Verlita said, "Vera, Vera Sanchez. How ya doin'?" and the two of them turned away talking.

D.H. stared at Verlita. What did she mean, Vera Sanchez? Who the hell was she trying to kid? Vera Sanchez. The rage burned up inside him, rankling, prickling, stickly and hot. A high buzzing whine sounded inside him. Liar. Two-bit liar. He knew her. He recognized her. He'd known her all his life, she couldn't go acting like he hadn't.

"Vera Sanchez," D.H. said out loud, slowly, holding the words careful inside his mouth. "Vera Sanchez."

Verlita and the squirrel hunter turned toward him.

"Look here a minute, Vera *San* chez," D.H. said.

She was watching him.

"Hot in here, ain't it?" and D.H. reached up and swept the hat off his head.

D.H. said her name then, said Verlita McHenry, but the sound of it was lost in the rasp of the rattles and the gasps and the music and the shouts all around. Verlita never screamed. She just stared at the top of his head with her eyes open, perfect white circles of shocked recognition, and D.H. never knew if she heard him or not.

"Get that fool idiot out of here!" and "Look out, look out now!" and "Keep back, little lady, that's a goddamn rattlesnake, can't you see it?" and "Sonuvabitch's drunk as a lord."

D.H. reached up with one hand.

"Watch it, he's got the sonuvabitch by the neck."

"Wouldja look at that."

"Sonuvabitch's crazy."

"Step back y'all, keep back. Lady, I hate to say it, but you're asking for it."

"Clarence, get back there and call the law."

D.H. watched Verlita.

Her bones were still. She stared at the rattler. D.H. held it up to her draped sideways, sagging some in the middle, one of his hands grasping the back of its head, the other lifting the vibrating end. He held it like the gift of a necklace.

Verlita looked for a long time, and then she reached out her hand. She touched the rattlesnake in the middle, ran a finger along the dry silky scales of its underbelly.

The men all went crazy, shouting, "*Lady!* Good god, woman!

Lady, listen here, look out now, you believe it? the bitch's asking
for it. Get her out of here, she's drunk as he is. That's a goddamn
*rattle*snake, ma'am, are you nuts?"

The rattler was dull, slate-colored in the dim lights, its chevron
markings blotchy except where they turned black and solid near
the tail. The dark sliver of tongue flicked in and out quickly,
continuously, smelling the room. The hiss of the rattles was unceasing, but D.H. held the snake firm, uncoiled, unable to strike.

"Put your hand there under it," he said softly, "They like their
middle supported, that's part of their nature." D.H. shook his
head. "Don't know why that is."

Verlita laughed. Then she did what none of them could abide,
and the room went suddenly silent. Even the jukebox ground
down into silence, and the only sound in the lounge of the Holiday
Inn was the dry hissing sound of the rattles, like the high buzzing
whine of an insect.

Verlita had put her hand around the middle of the rattlesnake's
belly, holding it in her fist, and her eyes turned upward to look
at D.H.

At once D.H. saw her. He knew exactly what was inside her.
He knew she was suspended in wonder, thinking nothing, knowing nothing but wonder at the strength of the snake's belly. Not
the fact of the smooth dryness, not the fact of the warmth from
where it'd been under the hat, but the sheer muscular force of
that belly that, going nowhere, moved restless, powerful, resist-
less inside her hand.

"It's—" Verlita shook her head, looking back at the snake,
watching it move and not move under her hand. "It's . . ." and
the breath burst out of her lungs in quick release. She laughed
again, throaty, wonderful, like it was a wonderful old joke, and
looked up at D.H.

Her eyes never blinked, never flinched, never moved away from
him. D.H. felt like it was his own fist around the rattlesnake's
belly. He felt the surprise and wonder running through his arm,

the same awe at the impossible strength, the same joy he'd suf-
fered himself the first time.

She knows me, D.H. thought. Yes, she knows me. Maybe she
don't know I'm Dwayne Henry DeWitt, but that woman knows
who I am. Verlita laughed again. They stood watching each other
in the smoke and the stink of stale liquor and the buzz of the
rattles and the low rumbling of men's voices, until the lights went
bright and the grumbling rose louder and there was the thick
clatter of boots on the stairs.

D.H. looked up at the sheriff thumping down the stairs with
three town cops behind him, looked down once at the rattler and
saw its tongue slowed, saw the slow meaningful flickering as it
confirmed where Verlita was standing, felt himself motionless,
paralyzed, and then the rattler whipped loose from his hand.

It happened so fast D.H. couldn't feel how it happened. Just
one second holding the neck tight and the next second shouts
and curses and Verlita screaming out one quick short fierce
scream and the rattler writhing fast away from him across the
floor. Then there were gun shots, a half dozen gun shots one
after the other, and D.H. leaned back against the bar trying to
will himself sober, moving his tongue against his teeth and blinking and breathing deep breaths. He thought then how his mama
always used to weep and mouth at him and tell him how whiskey
and rattlers was a terrible bad mix, and he thought how he probably shouldn't have had those last few Wild Turkey doubles, and
he thought, what a waste, when he saw how the rattler was shot
all to pieces because now the skin was worthless, just a mangled
useless bloody mess, and he thought, when he saw Verlita holding
her thumb out in front of her and crying, don't y'all get so excited,
a rattler's bite ain't no more worse than a flu shot, 'specially a
little old three-footer like that.

It wasn't until he was standing in the parking lot breathing in
the hot thick night air, when he saw the ambulance pull up and

the red flashing lights sweeping around and around in a circle and he saw Verlita walk out the door holding her thumb out in front of her, clutched in the closed fist of her other hand, and her eyes black circles like a coon's from running mascara and her not even looking at him, not looking around for him, before she got into the back of the ambulance, shrugging off the attendant trying to help her and climbing in by herself—it wasn't till that moment that D.H. realized he'd lost Verlita McHenry forever.

It all turned familiar then, so that when they pushed him into the back seat of the police cruiser he recognized the feeling, like he'd been pushed there a thousand times. The black sky over Oklahoma gliding by outside the window with only the dim hint of stars in the haze, the sickness rolling over him, the image of Verlita's face with the black circles of mascara were like memories of old memories of dreams.

It was even familiar when he leaned over to vomit, pain jabbing his kidneys, teeth and eyes and neck muscles cringing, and he reached up with one hand, because of the burning prickling sensation, reached inside his shirt above his left nipple and felt with the tips of his fingers the two little bloodless holes punctured over his heart.

1986

Mr. Sanger didn't answer nor make any response whatsoever when Eunice Mabry tapped on the screen and called out "Mr. Sanger? Mr. Sanger?" in her high nasal voice. She listened for him to tell her to come on in if he was open, but all she heard was a radio playing somewhere in the back. Eunice cupped her hands around the rims of her glasses and peered through the screen. If Mr. Sanger didn't mean to have customers surely he wouldn't have left the wooden door standing open and the yellow clockface turned face-front on the screen with its cardboard hands torn off and the black block letters underneath spelling out OPEN plain as day.

"Mr. Sanger!" Eunice hollered, and then jumped and jerked her head over her shoulder to look, but the highway behind her was empty. She took a step back from the screen door. Sanger's Auction Barn rose cockeyed above her, part tin-and-tarpaper, part wood. It sprawled for half an acre in either direction alongside the highway. Junk of varying natures and ages and proportions spread like creeping ivy along the porch and spilled out into the empty side lot where the old gas station used to be. There were no people anywhere around, just Stump Wilson's fat gray-headed beagle waddling along the drainage ditch with its nose to the ground. Eunice stepped to the screen again and pushed her lips close to it. "Mr. Sanger!" she whispered loudly. "You open, Mr. Sanger? You home?"

She strained to hear an answer through the dullness like cotton wadding in her ears. Well, Eunice Mabry's hearing might not be as good as some people's but it was not nearly so poor as her husband Raymond tried to make out and she could surely hear that radio. It was Ferlin Husky singing. If nothing else, Mr. Sanger was home, that much was fact. Eunice pulled open the screen. The cowbells overhead jerked on their strings and clanged together—and Eunice heard *that* perfectly well too— and then quieted down, and Eunice could hear Ferlin Husky clearer than ever, singing, "On the wings of a sno-o-ow whi-i-te dove, He sends his pu-u-ure, swe-e-et love." She took that for a sign. Glancing one quick time up and down the glaring hot high- way behind her, Eunice Mabry walked on in.

Sanger's was dark and smelled like a storm cellar. A shiver slid over Eunice as she passed from the stark sunlight into the auction barn. It was a strange thing to come by Sanger's alone on a Sunday morning. She couldn't even recollect the last time she'd been inside, although she might sit outside in the pickup as often as once a month while her husband combed Sanger's for just the right bit to fit an old horse harness or some rusted part to fix the hay baler. She stood inside the door and waited for the black jumble of shapes to take on some sense in the darkness.

A light was on in the little tin camping trailer Mr. Sanger used for an office and home. The trailer sat back in the far right-hand corner, enclosed in the high dank walls of the barn. Eunice smelled something cooking, bacon grease frying, stabbing salty and sharp through the mildew. She thought Mr. Sanger must be cooking himself breakfast. Then she remembered it was past eleven o'clock, too late in the morning for breakfast and too early for lunch. "Mr. Sanger?" Eunice called, and turned her good ear toward the trailer. She heard nothing but a choir on the radio now, singing "The Old Rugged Cross." Lord, she thought, what if that old man is dead and it would be just my luck to be the one to come along and find him. "Mr. Sanger?" she said again, not so loud, but the empty sound of her own voice stranded in the air of the barn made her feel foolish.

Well. I'm not going to just stand here in the dark talking to myself, she thought. He's open or he ain't, he's alive or else not. The best thing for me to do is look around and see if I can't find one of these spoon rings. She tilted her head back to peer through her glasses. The dark humping shapes slowly dissolved into objects, and as her eyes adjusted to the darkness, Eunice stood perfectly still inside the door and stared.

Every inch of Sanger's auction barn was covered with something. Old inner tubes hung in rows along the ceiling like strung-up black doughnuts, and behind or in front of the black doughnuts hung old sickles and saddles, tractor seats, harnesses, window fans, and milk crates. Every wall was crisscrossed with shelving, and on the shelves sat books and plates and crochet thread and jelly glasses, plastic flowers, plastic vases, faded silk pillowcases embroidered to "Mother" that soldiers had sent home during World War II. What places on the wall not covered with shelving were covered with pictures: photographs of Cedar when it was still Indian Territory, the men—white men and Indians—lined up in front of the high sidewalks on Main Street in battered cowboy hats, suit coats, and white shirts. Pictures of soldiers in uniform and skinny young basketball players (Eunice knew some of those faces—most of them dead now) crowded around their coach, all reaching down to lay a hand on the ball. Pictures of the Last Supper and the Dionne quintuplets, brides and hangings, baptisms and ground-breakings, dogs and horses and churches and birds.

Eunice took a step forward. Tables concocted out of planks and sawhorses took up all the floor space, with only little footpaths left in between. Well, she thought, if there's a spoon ring in this mess, I don't guess it'll be hanging from the ceiling. She edged along a narrow aisleway and bent her head to look at the contents of the nearest table. But on the table sat too many more books, more plastic flowers and vases, beaded necklaces and earbobs, ashtrays, old mixers, toy train engines, hurricane lamps and piggy banks and shoes. Every table was crowded with the same type of conglomeration. Eunice knew that with her weary eyes it'd take half a day to find what she'd come after. The urgency of time sliding past and Brother Packer now commencing his sermon in the church down the street nipped a small bite of panic inside Eunice's belly.

"Mr. Sanger!" she called out loudly into the mildewed and bacon-greased darkness. "Mr. Sanger, it's me, Eunice Mabry! Hate to bother you but I just come by to see if you was open or not!"

He started partway awake, fingers kneading the air, clutching for something that kept falling away. His lips fluttered, flew rapidly, fell still. He reached again, closed his fingers, but still it kept falling. Mr. Sanger wasn't ready. He hadn't had time yet to look at the inventory, didn't know what numbers to call out to begin, and nobody could hear him because the microphone kept falling and the estate couldn't be got rid of, would just pile up and up forever, because he didn't know the numbers and his tongue was clotted against the roof of his mouth, until he knew it was a dream and came on awake but could not open his eyes.

"Mother?" he said into the brightness, and then he remembered and saw her in the white bed and white sheets, and the clear tubing crawling into her nostrils and the machine beside her with the pump rising and falling inside the glass. Then he remembered past that and closer than that, and the weight fell down again, weighed down upon him, and he opened his eyes in the light.

The Choctaw woman had left the radio up too loud, and even from across the room this way he could see she'd left the lid off the lard can again. The sight of that lidless lard can on the counter filled him with such a power of grief and self-pity that he started to cry.

"Truth is, Mr. Sanger," the Mabry woman said, "much as I hate to tell it . . ." She lifted her head and her eyes swam toward him, magnified like minnows behind the thick wall of her glasses. "Truth is"—her voice dropped to the strange whisper that seemed to drift into the world through her nose—"my girl's took off again."

Mr. Sanger looked at her, trying to place which girl it was. Seemed to him like Raymond Mabry had fathered a whole parcel of children, mixed male and female, redheaded to the last one, just like their daddy, sufficient to fill up the wagon on Saturday mornings in town. He didn't know which girl this woman was talking about. "Which girl's that, ma'am?" he said.

"Why, my daughter, Mr. Sanger, the only girl I got." The whisper snaked lower like she was telling women's secrets that ought not to be told out loud. "Only *child* I got, only one I got born to me." She rocked her head side to side and then suddenly lowered it and looked down at the busy fingers in her lap.

The gauze fluttered and parted, and Mr. Sanger recollected that it wasn't Raymond Mabry who'd owned all those children but his father, old Anderson Mabry, dead thirty years now, and Raymond himself had been one of those redheaded kids in the back. The weight pressed down harder, crawled all inside him, and the sore on his leg kicked up its ache. He reached with both hands and picked up his leg to settle it higher on the pillow. "Could you . . ." he said to the woman, but then he forgot what he wanted. His eyes drifted to the lard can, and the tears choked up again. "Sister," he said, "could you reach me that spit can? I don't like to trouble people but I can't get up. This leg here . . ." And he looked down at the piece of him that didn't belong to him but crippled him anyhow and caused so much pain. But when he looked up again the woman was still watching her fingers and didn't appear to have heard him, and in another moment Mr. Sanger forgot what he'd said.

"The reason I come by is on account of my daughter."

Mr. Sanger was quiet, looking at the Mabry woman's slow-twisting fingers. She lifted her head and the overhead bulb flashed on her glasses, and then she leaned toward him and the huge eyes swelled and filled up the space. "She's took off from

another one of these husbands of hers, last night was a week
ago, and Mr. Sanger, I don't know what to tell you but I don't
aim for it to happen again." She sat back in the chair and folded
her hands.

"Wasn't you a Newell? From down by Burnt Cabin?" Mr. Sanger said.

Eunice watched his face a minute, then she leaned toward him
again and tilted her head.

"Said wasn't you a Newell, or kin to them Newells? From down
by Burnt Cabin. Jed Newell and them."

"My daddy's Chub Blankenship, Mr. Sanger." She thought
sure Mr. Sanger knew that. "I'm a Holloway on my mother's side,
but there's only about six of us left."

"No, I reckon not. You just kindly look like them," Mr. Sanger
said. "Holloway. I know the Holloways. Used to know the Holloways. There's not many of them left." Mr. Sanger's eyes wandered to the lard can again.

"I don't like people to know it. That's how come me to come
by on a Sunday, Mr. Sanger, I'll have to apologize for that." She
leaned toward him again. "But it's the Lord's own truth and
there's no sense Raymond Mabry pretending like it ain't."

"No sir," Mr. Sanger said, and his voice trembled with sorrow
and emotion, "it's no use to pretend like anything ain't."

"No sir. That's true. I told him that. I've told him time and
again. He'd just as soon stick his head in the mud and let them
children starve or get raised by their daddy or no telling what,
but I don't aim to see it and I told him that in no uncertain
terms."

Mr. Sanger saw the parcel of redheaded children crowded in
the back of the wagon again. He saw the old man turn around
with the butt end of the whip in his hand and whop one of the
children on the back of the ear. He saw the child tune up to bawl.
Mr. Sanger felt he might be ready to cry himself, and he said,
"No, you can't leave them children on the mercy of their daddy.

I was a good daddy, I loved them boys. But boys needs a . . .
children needs a . . ." Mr. Sanger went ahead crying.

Eunice got up from the kitchen chair where she sat across
from him and pulled a handful of pink Kleenex loose from the
box on the back of the divan. A putrid smell, vaguely familiar,
cut through the odor of bacon grease and drifted around her, and
Eunice handed the Kleenex to Mr. Sanger and hurried to sit back
down.

"They do," she said, "they do, all children do. Well, I have tried.
But I'm raising that batch from her first marriage and I can't do
any more. I'm too old. I told Raymond that and I told Raymodeen
that when she started wailing around about this ring. But do you
think they listen to me? They act like I'm nothing but . . . nothing
but a foolish old woman, on account of"—Eunice dropped her
head, and the words came slow and shamed from her lips—"how
easy . . . it is . . . to talk behind my back."

"I had six boys. You knew I had six boys? At one time I did.
Two of them got killed in the war. Within a day of each other.
Isn't that strange?"

Mr. Sanger watched the woman, waiting for some kind of reaction. It was one of the more powerful coincidences in his life
and seldom failed to get a reaction from whoever he told it to.
His two youngest sons, brothers right next to each other, not but
fourteen months between them, and one of them got killed in
France and turn right around, the next day—only who knew if it
was the next day, might have been the same day the way time
warps and changes in travel and today might be tomorrow in
China, they said that all the time on the news—turn right around,
halfway around the world, the other one gets killed on some little
useless island by the Japs. It was a strange business. But the
Mabry woman was looking in her lap again and did not look up to
share Mr. Sanger's notion about what a strange business it was.

"Raymond thinks it'll learn her a lesson," Eunice said. "Says
if she gets hungry enough she'll go home. That's what I keep

trying to tell him. She's never done a lick of public work in her life and she's not about to know how to start now. I tell him and tell him: it don't make a bit of difference, she'll just write her another letter, don't you know that?"

"She'll just write her another letter," Mr. Sanger said.

"Yes, and get her another husband and have her some more kids and then run off from him. I can't raise any more of her children, Mr. Sanger, I'm too old to mess with the ones I got now. Raymond says he wishes he'd never learnt her reading and writing. I told him it's not so much the reading causes the trouble, but that writing, mister, is a danger which no fool ought to never get learnt. Raymond says if he'd just had a son he'd have sent that one to school and kept Raymodeen home, schooling never did a thing in the world for that girl but fill her head with fool notions. Sure never did teach her how to work. Taught her how to write these blamed letters is all *I* can see. She got that first one out of the army, well, I didn't mind him so much, but that second one, Lord, I don't know where she got him."

Eunice could not look at Mr. Sanger's face, it seemed like so personal a telling, but the need of it was jammed up inside her and she had to go on.

"I think she gets these names out of a magazine or something. That second one come from clear down in Florida or someplace. And that's not the worst of it, Mr. Sanger. This last one, I'm ashamed to tell it, this last one come out of—*McAlester*. That's how bad it's got." Eunice shook her head.

"I used to have some people down around McAlester. He any kin to the Tannehills from around there?"

"What's that?"

"Said, is this fellow any kin to the Tannehills down there?"

"No sir. He don't come *from* McAlester. He come *out* of there, come out of the *prison*, Mr. Sanger. That's the kind of thing I'm having to contend with here."

"Well," Mr. Sanger said. He tried to recollect which one of Raymond Mabry's sons might have wound up in prison, but he couldn't seem to put a face to the notion of Raymond Mabry ever having had any sons. He pulled a matchstick out of his shirt pocket and used it to scratch the sore place inside his ear that never would seem to heal up or go away.

"And I don't aim to see those children raised up by a convict, I don't care if he *is* their daddy. Well, she just took off and left him Saturday was a week ago and left those two babies in the bed. *I* don't know how come her to not have any more sense than that. She's got this thing in her mind about this spoon ring and you can't talk a lick of sense into her. I spent more money than I even care to think about, trying. She's down at Fort Smith, at the Salvation Army, and if that's not pitiful I don't know what is."

"At the Salvation Army," said Mr. Sanger.

"Well, yes, and you can imagine about how long *that's* going to last."

"Down at Fort Smith?"

"It might not be so bad if you could trust her to stay put and not commence writing any more letters—"

"Did I ever show you this?" Mr. Sanger grunted and pulled himself up on the divan. He reached behind him and took a wooden plaque with a gold plate down off the wall. "Look at this here," he said and handed the plaque to Eunice Mabry.

Eunice pulled the plaque close to her face. The engraving on the gold plate, when she could finally make it out, said:

James Hardwell "Cotton" Sanger
In Recognition Of A Lifetime Of Achievement
Issued 1972
ARKANSAS AUCTIONEERS ASSOCIATION
FORT SMITH, ARKANSAS

"Yes sir," Eunice said, and handed the plaque back to Mr. Sanger. "That's nice, ain't it?"

Mr. Sanger held the plaque in his lap and stared at it.

"But what I know is," Eunice said, "what I keep trying to tell my husband, she'll just get her some more names somewhere and start writing letters. She's not about to stay at the Salvation Army forever. She's not about to go to work. There's nothing for it but for her to get herself another husband, and Lord she has already scraped the bottom of the barrel as it is."

"Did you know that at one time folks called me Cotton?"

"What's that?"

"Cotton. Did you know that everybody in this county—no ma'am, everybody in this state and half of Arkansas and Texas —called me Cotton at one time?"

It was a wonder to Mr. Sanger that once he'd been so young and brash and familiar, once he'd had such a head of white-blond hair, that folks all around had known him only as Cotton. He'd been Mr. Sanger for such a great many years now, Mr. Sanger to everybody from the sheriff and the preacher and Dr. Hawkins on down, that it seemed strange to even remember himself as Cotton. And then again, the fact that he'd lived so long as to become mister to the whole world was strange in itself.

Eunice strained to hear what-all Mr. Sanger was saying. She heard *cotton* and *county* and *Arkansas* and *Texas,* and then the word *cotton* again. She had some vague notion about auctioneers auctioning off cotton, though she hadn't heard tell of it in a long time. She thought Mr. Sanger might have got that plaque for auctioning off a lot of cotton.

"Yes sir," she said, "that's real nice. Well see, Mr. Sanger, now here it is. If I can get Raymodeen to go back home to this husband, I can quit worrying about them babies. I got no use for the man, that is true, but every one she's come up with has been worse than the last and I shudder to think what she might come up with next." She leaned closer to Mr. Sanger, not wanting to say these last words too loud. "Truth is, she's getting a little long in the tooth. She writes these letters and sends off her high school graduation picture and I admit she does look pretty in that picture but Lord she graduated high school in 1966 and she don't look a thing like that now." She let her voice drop a little lower. "You see what I'm saying, Mr. Sanger. Any man takes up with a woman and marries her on the basis of a 1966 high school graduation picture is not the kind of man you want raising your grandkids."

Mr. Sanger pulled his eyes away from the plaque and turned them on the Mabry woman when he heard the word *grandkids*.

"And I can't take them two littlest ones to raise. Even if I could, there's no guarantee there wouldn't be others come along if Raymodeen got half a chance, I don't care if she is nearly forty years old. Some women are just outfitted to bear babies—"

She stopped, and dropped her eyes to the fidgeting fingers in her lap.

"Anyhow," she said after a bit, "being fit by the Lord to get pregnant at the drop of a hat don't make a person fit to raise 'em, if you know what I—" She stopped herself again, shocked that she would have said such a thing. She raised her eyes to see if Mr. Sanger did indeed know what she meant. He was looking at her with watery, red-rimmed eyes.

"How many grandkids you got, Miz Mabry?" he said.

"Seven all told, Mr. Sanger, counting the one that's in Florida."

"Got seventeen myself. Ain't that something?" He shook his head in amazement. The plaque slipped from his hands and lay unattended on his lap. "Seventeen grandkids, nine great-grandkids, and—you can believe this or not, Miz Mabry—I truthfully have got three great-great-grandkids. Three of 'em. They all come out of Earnest. He got started early and every one of his did too. Wait a minute. I got a picture around here somewhere."

Mr. Sanger struggled to get up, but the pain sliced through his leg and slapped him back down. He lay staring up at the brightness, both hands wrapped around his knee, squeezing it like maybe he could squeeze that foreigner pain back down to his shinbone. It ought to stay down there in the part of him that didn't belong to him, quit sliding up like it belonged in his body someplace.

"Raymodeen got started late herself," Eunice said softly. "I guess we can be grateful for that." She hated to think how many kids Raymodeen'd have strung around the country by now if she'd got started early like it looked like her daughter Darlene was fixing to do. The thought of Darlene in her tight feisty bluejeans discomfited Eunice so badly that she stood up and walked over to the icebox. She had reached out a hand and laid it on the door handle before she came to herself. She jerked her hand back and turned around to Mr. Sanger.

"Can I get you anything, Mr. Sanger? You need a cold drink of water or anything while I'm up?" She wrapped her hand inside the fold of her skirt.

Mr. Sanger looked around the four walls of the trailer. There had been something he'd wanted, but he couldn't now think what it might have been. "No, sister," he said after a while. "No, I don't think so."

It occurred to Eunice then to wonder how Mr. Sanger got along, with that festered leg so ugly it looked like he'd be hard put to get up off the divan. She thought about the bacon grease she'd smelled when she first came in. She couldn't now distinguish the scent of bacon grease from the snuff smell and old man smell coming from Mr. Sanger and that other smell, the sickly sweet putrid one that drifted past her now and again, but there was still the sense in the air of food having been cooked there. She looked around the kitchen and saw dishes stacked in the dish drain and an open Crisco can on the counter. "Mr. Sanger," she said, "is somebody tending you?"

"Miz Mabry . . ." Mr. Sanger began, and then he let out a slow terrible sigh like it was useless to even begin to think about talking about it, and shut his eyes.

"Are you doing for yourself?" Come to think of it, Eunice couldn't fathom how that old man could get up off the divan and get to the bathroom, much less cook himself a meal. "Have they got somebody coming in for you? Mr. Sanger?"

He just lay there with his eyes shut, shaking his head.

Eunice tried to think what she'd heard around town about Mr. Sanger, if the Senior Citizens was delivering to him or not. She put her hand back to the icebox and opened it and looked in. There was a head of lettuce and a quart of milk, a jar of apple juice, a little dab of broccoli on a plate, and a bowl of stewed prunes. There were eggs in the door and a hunk of government cheese and a half dozen Tupperware containers filled with what looked to be casserole food or stew. She shut the icebox and bent over the dish drain to look closer. Those dishes were clean. Satisfied that somebody was indeed coming in to do for him, Eunice's thoughts dropped away from Mr. Sanger and turned back onto the worn track they'd been running in for a week.

"What I come by for," she said, and eased over to her chair and sat down, "I hate to bother you on Sunday, I wouldn't for the world want to do that, but I'm just now seeing my way clear what to do about this situation, and Raymond says if I don't aim to go down there this afternoon I can just forget about him taking me, he's got to hay all next week."

Still Mr. Sanger lay perfectly quiet with his eyes closed.

"He thinks I'm at church now. He dropped me off there this morning."

Eunice bit down on her own lip. She hadn't meant to tell Mr. Sanger that. She eyed Mr. Sanger, waiting for a reaction to her deceit. She could hardly believe it herself. Eunice Mabry wasn't a woman to go around lying to her husband, but she had to admit that, in fact, this very morning, and on a Sunday no less, she'd lied to him in deed if not in so many words. She expected Mr. Sanger to be shocked, but Mr. Sanger didn't move, didn't blink an eye, hardly appeared to even be breathing.

"He'd skin me alive if he knew I come by here, Mr. Sanger," Eunice said, watching his face, shamed and half proud of being such a deceitful woman, "but I don't know what else to do. He's intent on learning Raymodeen a lesson and Raymodeen's intent on this ex-con husband of hers buying her this ring. I don't know what that convict's intent on but he sure hadn't come up with a ring yet and looks to me like he don't intend to."

Eunice leaned forward in her chair. She thought maybe Mr. Sanger had fallen asleep.

"Well," she said, lifting her voice and ignoring the little jabs at her conscience for bothering an old man during his nap, "Raymond'll be back at the church house twelve o'clock to pick me up. See. That's my problem here, Mr. Sanger. Truth is, I haven't got all that much time."

Mr. Sanger let go with a little shuddering sound out of his mouth and opened his eyes. He looked up at Eunice, and she could see how cloudy and wet his eyes were, could see he'd been laying there crying the whole time.

"None of us—" he said, and choked up till he couldn't say anything and had to shut his eyes again.

Eunice felt bad. Here she'd come and upset this old man on a Sunday and she didn't even know what in particular he was upset about. She sat watching Mr. Sanger cry, her stomach pinched up with fidgets. Things looked to be worse than she'd thought. No talk in the town had told her how bad Mr. Sanger was failing. A clock on the kitchen wall shaped like a giant Coca-Cola bottle cap revealed that time and the world were pushing relentlessly on towards twelve o'clock, and Eunice was no closer to getting her spoon ring than when she'd walked in the door.

"I'm just going to have to go out there and find it myself," she said, standing up, more certain than ever that one lay hidden in the chaos of the auction barn somewhere. She immediately sat back down. What was a spoon ring? Eunice didn't know what one looked like. Her only experience with rings was the worn-thin gold band she wore on her hand that matched the one Raymond Mabry kept locked in his tackle box along with the U.S. Savings Bonds he'd bought during the War. Raymodeen had one like that, had several in fact, plus an engagement ring inlaid with three little rhinestones this last good for nothing husband had sent in the mail from the McAlester State Prison. It couldn't be anything like that Raymodeen wanted. Eunice thought about spoons and what they might have to do with it. She pictured tablespoons and teaspoons and long-handled ice tea spoons like the ones in her silverware drawer at home, but she couldn't imagine how they could have anything to do with the type of ring that Raymodeen would have her mind so set on she'd leave another husband over it. A spoon ring must be something mighty precious.

"Mr. Sanger!" she burst out suddenly, the need like a drumming inside her that drowned out any sense of manners or pity for an old man weeping to himself on the divan. "If you could just explain a spoon ring to me, tell me what I'm looking for, I'll go see if I can't try and find it myself!"

She got up and went to Mr. Sanger and gave his shoulder a little shake.

Mr. Sanger opened his eyes. His cheeks were wet.

"I don't mean to bother you," Eunice said, "I hate to bother you, I really do, but this situation is more than a mortal woman can stand. I'm sixty-five years old, Mr. Sanger. I got four children in my house under the age of fourteen. That oldest girl Darlene is wild as a cotton planter, I hate to say it, she's going to wind up no telling how. She sasses me and backtalks me, never gives me a minute's peace, and the littlest one still wets the bed, he's going on nine years old, and them two middle ones holler and beat on each other and run a person crazy from daylight to dark.

I don't know where Raymodeen got this notion about this ring
—I never once in my life did know where that girl got a notion
and she's had a flat hundred of 'em—I don't even know where
she ever heard of such a thing, but she's been after this convict
husband of hers to buy her one for a solid month now and she
hadn't quit yet and she's not going to quit till she either gets
what she wants or ends up divorced. If she ends up divorced,
Mr. Sanger, I'm going to end up with those two least ones of
hers to raise, and them two are worse than the whole rest of 'em
put together and I say that even if I am their own grandma and
love them dearly but I just lay it off to them having half convict
blood."

"You knew my wife passed away, didn't you?"

Eunice stopped still, confused, her heart galloping ahead and
her mind brought up short. She stared down at him. Mr. Sanger's
wife had been dead for five or six years.

"She had a stroke, Miz Mabry. She had a whole series of them,
but it was that last stroke that finally took her." Mr. Sanger rubbed
the pink wad of Kleenex over his eyes and shuddered, his breath
ragged as knuckles on a washboard. "That woman was a big
woman when she went into the hospital and when she died she
weighed eighty-three pounds. Same size as her ten-year-old
granddaughter." He looked up at Eunice. "Isn't that strange?"

Mr. Sanger watched the face of the woman standing over him.
Her mouth hung open a little, and her eyes swam huge and wild
behind her glasses. Her hair puffed out, lit from above like a halo.
He thought that here was a woman who could understand truly
what a strange business life was. How strange, in particular,
Cotton Sanger's own life had been. He nodded his head at her.

"It goes by fast, don't it?" he said.

"Mr. Sanger?" Eunice whispered. "Are you listening to me?
I'm trying to tell you I need help here."

The woman hovered over him, waiting to hear him. Mr. Sanger
hoisted himself higher on the divan.

"I had to quit going to funerals," he said. "You knew that, I guess? I quit not long after Jewell passed away. Oh, just seemed like I couldn't stop thinking about everything. At a funeral it'd hit me all at once." He wiped his eyes. "Started that right after she first went in the hospital. She laid in the bed eight months and twenty-two days, did you know it? Shrunk to the size of a ten-year-old."

Mr. Sanger struggled to draw all the different parts of it together so he could explain it to this woman. He wrapped his fingers around his knee and squeezed.

"Nowdays it's liable to hit me all at once any time of the day or night. Matter of fact," he said, watching the woman's halo shimmer and quiver, "seems like it just stays with me all the time. Never goes away. I just lay here and picture all of it. You know what I mean?"

Eunice lifted her voice again, twisting her hands together, staring down at him. "I never asked for help in my life, Mr. Sanger, nor told a soul my private troubles, but this situation has got me completely out of hand."

Her hands and heart were shaking, her voice vibrating, and then the words exploded from her, and she didn't know where they came from.

"My husband's going to kill me, Mr. Sanger! If he comes to pick me up at the church house and I'm not standing in that parking lot, I can't even begin to imagine what he's liable to do. I got to get this spoon ring and get back there and I mean right this minute!"

"It's hard, not going to funerals," Mr. Sanger answered. "Well, there's one about every week, ain't they? That's all we do in this town, go to funerals. Don't it seem like that to you? But I just had to quit it. I'd be standing at the graveside—or this is how it started, at least—I'd be standing there looking at the green tarp they've taken to spreading over the mound lately like they could hide it's dirt and rocks under there anyhow—and all of a sudden

I'd be six or seven years old in the coldcellar at my granny's house getting ready to hand a cake of butter up to my mama."

He paused to feel for a minute that hot morning and the light like a glaring sulfur square behind the shape of his mother and the smell inside the coldcellar like the smell of the very heart of the earth itself.

Dear Lord, Eunice thought, Mr. Sanger has gone plumb senile. Nobody had told her Mr. Sanger had gone senile.

"Or then again I might be ten or twelve laying in the back of the wagon watching the stars jump every time the wagon bumps and the sky black like it's never so black now. Or I might be nineteen that time me and Jewell come all the way back from Ferris pumping that little switchman's railroad cart, stole that little red cart or just borrowed it really, and pumped it every foot of the way on them tracks from Ferris to Cedar because they'd sent word her sister Irene was having her baby."

He studied the back-lit face of the woman standing over him.

"My granny's house was in Mississippi. Before we all come here in a wagon. Before all us white people come here."

He felt sure the woman shared his own amazement.

"That was another *century,* ma'am. Isn't that something?"

Mr. Sanger shook his head.

"Started out it'd be the same pictures all the time. Them three I just told you about, two or three others. It was like somebody'd just push a button in my head. I'd be inside it and outside it both, like you'll do in a dream. Like that time me and Jewell come back from Ferris. If that one played, why, I'd feel what it felt like on the inside, how hot we got and it was a cold day in November, feel that handle wearing blisters in my palm, see Jewell's face across from me, red and sweaty and about half mad because she'd never wanted to go over to Ferris in the first place, it was my people we'd gone to visit. But I'd see it on the outside too. On the inside I'd feel how huge and heavy that cart was, how much work it took when we come to a hill, and on the outside

I'd see this little red rusted wood and iron cart and these two just-married kids pumping that handle up and down, up and down, trying to get there before that baby did. Making good time, too. You'd be surprised.

"Afterwhile, though, it turned the corner on me. It wouldn't just be one or two things. It'd be everything. I couldn't stop it. I'd see bad things, terrible things, just as well as the good. I'd see that colored man they lynched when I was a boy and set fire to him and tied him to a wagon and drug him, whipped up them horses and drug that burnt body right through the town. All the men laughing. Body was pink in places where the skin had burnt off and hadn't cooked black again. Looked like a white man. Little charred stumps where his hands and feet ought to of been."

Mr. Sanger rolled sideways a little, turned his head on the pillow, his mouth loose like it was filling up with spit. He wiped the pink Kleenex over his lips.

"I'd see that lieutenant standing at the screen door out yonder with that yellow envelope in his hand and Jewell wouldn't let him in. She stood at the door shaking her head, had her hands crossed over her breasts, looking at the floor, shaking her head. Wouldn't let him in. He come back the next day, it was the exact same picture all over again. I stood at the rear of the store with the push broom in my hand, watching them. I had that feeling, you know? That feeling like whatever you're doing or seeing, you've already done it just like that once in your life only it was so long ago you forgot or else you dreamed it, you know that feeling? I don't know if other folks gets that feeling. I get it a lot. Used to get it a lot. And I had it that morning, only it come to me in a flash that it really had happened, just the day before. Just the very day before. And I thought first that lieutenant must be awful stupid, couldn't he remember he was just here yesterday? And then I thought maybe he'd forgot and left something here. Or wanted directions to some other poor citizen's house. Oh, I thought a lot of things. As many things as your mind'll let you think in the space of time it takes to catch up with what your gut already knows. My body already knew it was another one of my boys dead because I'd wet myself. Standing there with my hand on the push broom."

Mr. Sanger had to pause a minute to wipe his eyes. It was getting hard to see the woman. The light on the ceiling fractured and splintered, making rainbows, shooting off pinpoints like tiny white shooting stars.

"Afterwhile I might see anything at all at a funeral. I might see Jewell laying in the bed nursing one of our boys after it was first born and I might see one of them same boys half-grown and naked jumping in the water at Bluff Hole. Might feel myself starting off an auction one morning over in Arkansas, don't remember what town now or what year, just the sight of frost on the blades of an old brush hog and me turning around to ask somebody what time is it. I'd see that whipping tree they had out yonder, you remember that tree? Used to be a big red oak tree right out here where Main Street crosses the train tracks."

Mr. Sanger gestured toward the front of the store with his Kleenex, then used the tattered end of it to wipe his eyes.

"Choctaws used to use that tree for a whipping tree, though some folks'll try to tell you it was for council meetings and such but I know better. But what I'd see was the face of this one Indian man tied up, getting whipped there. If a man was guilty of something back then they'd either shoot him or else whip him with a bullwhip, that's how these Choctaws did, and I probably saw a dozen or more men whipped at that tree when I was a kid, but at a funeral it's just the face of this one man always appears to me. No good reason why. See, that's how strange this business is: some of these visions are of a more personal nature than I'd ever want to tell about, some of 'em don't hardly have anything to do with me at all. Just things I've seen."

He lay back with his eyes closed and let the images wash over

him. "Sister? You know that baby?" Mr. Sanger saw the baby
girl's screaming face poking out from under the feathertick,
Irene's freckled arm around her, and Jewell's face, Jewell's young
face, turning to look at him, furious as the squalling baby's because she'd missed the birthing of her sister's first child. "She
lived to be pretty near an old woman. She's already passed on."
He shook his head, defeated by such an unfolding of events. "I
watched her from cradle to coffin, and she was a white-headed
old woman when she went."

Eunice didn't know what in the world Mr. Sanger was talking
about. What baby? What white-headed old lady? She could only
make out about half of what he was saying, but words that came
through to her were *funeral* and *coffin, bullwhip* and *Choctaw,
jewel, century, coldcellar. Lieutenant. Burnt-black body. Push
broom* and *baby* and *strange.* She understood that Mr. Sanger's
mind was flat gone. She could see what a pitiful track he was
thinking in, how he was making up and dwelling on some terrible
ideas. Dwelling on coffins and gravesides was poor habit for
anybody.

"Don't talk like that now," she said, "dwelling on such kind of
things is no help." She clicked her tongue at him, her eyes on
the paneled wall above his head, studying the several rows of
framed family pictures. She tried to think how she might return
the topic of conversation to the business of spoon rings. "Listen!"
she said finally, loudly, bending over him, "I got to be going here
pretty quick, Mr. Sanger, couldn't you just—"

But the faint odor came to her again as she bent toward the
divan, and this time she placed it.

It was the same smell that wafted downwind from the crow
Raymond Mabry had shot a few weeks ago and hung up by one
claw on the wire fence where he fed his ducks. The dead crow
was a device to keep other crows from coming around to sneak-
eat the baby ducks' corn. Crows were smart. They knew death

of their own kind when they saw it, knew death when they smelled it, and when they recognized a death place they wouldn't come around.

Eunice straightened quickly, took a step back.

"It was awful good of you to come, ma'am." Mr. Sanger's damp eyes were open again, peering up at her. "Hardly nobody likes to come visit an old man. My boys comes by sometimes when they can get somebody to drive them, but Lord they're old men theirselves. It's good to have some regular company. Are you from the Senior Citizens?"

He looked up at her expectantly, waiting for an answer.

Eunice shook her head, staring down at him, feeling like she might be close to crying herself on account of the strain and the smell and the pitiful condition of Mr. Sanger's brain.

"Oh, this leg of mine's bothering me some," he said, "but outside of that I guess I'm getting along all right. That Indian woman comes in to clean does a pretty fair job, only she never can seem to remember to cover up that spit can, just the opposite to Jewell, she couldn't abide a uncovered spit can, but don't y'all fault her for that."

The woman's halo swayed side to side, now hiding the light on the ceiling, now letting it burst forth to glare into Mr. Sanger's pained eyes.

"Did they send you from the gover'ment?" Mr. Sanger felt certain this woman was here to help him but he couldn't for the life of him figure out who'd sent her. Still the halo kept swaying. Mr. Sanger shut his eyes against the light, but the presence of the woman stayed with him, hovering.

"Guess I'll be going now," Eunice said softly. She took a step back toward the door. "He'll be back at the church any minute. He's liable to whup me. He's liable to tear my hair out. He's got some pretty strong ideas." She hardly knew what she was saying.

Mr. Sanger reached out and grabbed a piece of her skirt. He pulled her toward him.

"Would you bend down here and hug me?" he said.

"Do what?"

"Said, would you bend down here and hug me. I can't get up."

A shiver slid over Eunice kin to the one that had passed over her when she'd first stepped in the auction barn door. Mr. Sanger had a powerful tight grip on her skirt. She reached a hand down and tried to pry his fingers loose, but his grip was as tight as a baby's. "Mr. Sanger!" she said, "Let go now, I got to get back, my husband is waiting for me!"

But Mr. Sanger held on, crying quietly, eyes closed and his cheeks streaming wet.

Eunice looked down at him. She saw him then, an old weeping wasted man, dying alone.

Strangely, like a vision, the cells in Mr. Sanger's face seemed to smooth out and rearrange themselves. His face changed, so she thought, to a young's man's, brash and familiar, the skin stretched tight over the bones, the sparse yellow hair gone white-blond and thick. Eunice blinked her weak eyes, passed her hand in front of her glasses, and Mr. Sanger's skin returned to parched tissue dampened with tear trails.

Suddenly, without knowing why or how, she bent from the waist and let him embrace her.

Mr. Sanger hugged her hard, wrapped his arms across her shoulders and pulled her down on top of him so that her torso lay across his and her knees jammed against the hard ledge of the divan.

Eunice felt Mr. Sanger's chest and belly swell up against her, felt his old breastbone and her breastbone touching each other and her flat withered breasts caught in between. She knew then, could feel it inside her, what a long dry age it had been since Mr. Sanger had been touched by another person. She knew how his skin ached for touching, how his bones and muscles felt gnawed inside like arthritis with a kind of empty hunger to be squeezed and held close. Her own belly and cheeks and back muscles answered, sagged loose and unresisting against him. Her body warmed, opened. She could not separate his need and comfort from her own.

At once Mr. Sanger pressed his palms flat against her back and spread his fingers, pressed her front all along the front of his chest, held her down against him as if he would press the length of her body inside his own.

Nausea and guilt choked up in her throat as it had fifty years before when the Duvall boys caught her at the spring house and tried to kiss her and pulled her drawers to her ankles and pushed her down in the mud. She struggled to stand up, but Mr. Sanger held her tighter. The putrid odor washed over her again. In Eunice's mind the blackened image of the dead crow thumped against the wire fence in the wind.

She kicked her feet in the air and struggled, but his palms pressed down harder. She wondered how she could not have understood that Mr. Sanger was already past dying. That his body had decayed and rotted before the soul even left. Eunice thought she might throw up all over him. She wedged her hand against Mr. Sanger's armpits, planted her knees against the front of the divan, and shoved back.

Mr. Sanger let her go with a sob.

Eunice heaved backward, nearly fell, caught herself, and stood finally in cold waves of revulsion and pity, looking down at him, shaking. He was crying again. Or still crying. Seemed like he'd been crying the whole morning long. Eunice began once again to back toward the camping trailer's front door.

"Thank you, ma'am." Mr. Sanger was gazing up at her, a soft, settled, unfocused look on his face. "I'm proud you come by to see me. Not many folks takes the time. Not many. . . ."

But Mr. Sanger's mind had strayed off again. His eyes drifted to the framed photographs covering the wall above him, wandered around the room, and settled finally on the Crisco can sitting open on the top of the kitchen counter.

Eunice turned and shoved on the trailer's front door.

For the space of a skipped heartbeat Eunice thought she was free.

In the next beat she saw she was not on the safe blacktop highway in front of Sanger's but standing in the lightless auction barn surrounded, enclosed, by the dense mat of objects, goods, dark unfathomable shapes. Daylight streamed through the screen door far away, on the far side of the barn. Eunice took a step toward it, stumbled against something, righted herself, rushed forward again. She hurried through the musty darkness, bumping into tables, thumping against crates. She looked neither right nor left. Her eyes focused on the bright sunlit square of the screen.